THE ISLAND

THE ISLAND

Antigone Kefala

TRANSIT
BOOKS

Published by Transit Books
1250 Addison St #103, Berkeley, CA 94702
www.transitbooks.org

© Antigone Kefala, 1984
Introduction © Madeleine Watts, 2025
ISBN: 979-8-89338-003-3 (paperback)
Cover design by Sarah Schulte | Typesetting by Transit Books
Printed in the United States of America

9 8 7 6 5 4 3 2 1

All rights reserved. This book or any portion thereof may not be reproduced or used in any manner whatsoever without the express written permission of the publisher except for the use of brief quotations in a book review.

 This project is supported in part by a grant from the National Endowment for the Arts.

To Mica

Introduction

The first time I heard about Antigone Kefala was when I was in my second year of university. She was described to me by an older writer as "a preeminent poet from Sydney." At the time, I was majoring in English at the University of Sydney, but Kefala's work had never been assigned, and most of the writers I associated with Sydney were long dead. I remember going to the bookstore just off campus that afternoon and browsing the shelves, but I couldn't find anything by Antigone Kefala, and quickly gave up the search.

This is not an uncommon story. Antigone Kefala was a writer who spent much of her literary career flying under the radar. In 2010, the same year that I first heard about her, Kefala wrote in her journal about being left out of the *Macquarie PEN Anthology of Australian Literature*. She was, understandably, upset that certain writers—she among them—had been "totally effaced." The anthology

I

INTRODUCTION

included work by early British settlers, excerpts of nineteenth century drudgery, and Kefala's contemporaries, like David Malouf, Shirley Hazzard, and Gerald Murnane. In an interview with the literary journal *HEAT* around the same time, Kefala said, "I have been so far out of any critical line in Australia in terms of writing. Apart from one or two people, no one has approached the work as a serious intellectual activity." For a long time, it seemed like the only story to tell about Antigone Kefala was a ghost story: her persistent absence from any mainstream literary recognition, in Australia, and elsewhere.

Antigone Kefala was born in the Romanian city of Brăila in 1931, a city on the Danube close to the modern-day Moldovan border. Kefala's parents were Greek by heritage, but her family had lived in Romania for three generations by the time their daughter was born. After World War II, as a wave of political unrest swept through Romania, the family fled. Kefala arrived in 1947, at age sixteen, in Greece, a country that was on the brink of civil war. The family lived in refugee camps set up by the International Refugee Organization, and set about applying to emigrate. Rejected by Australia because of an X-ray that showed a small shadow on her mother's lung, the family instead left for New Zealand in 1951. Later, Kefala described the shock of the green dampness of New Zealand, the difficulty of communicating in English, and the feeling of first being unwanted, "made to feel that our faces, our gestures, belonged to this outside category with which the locals did not want to become involved."

In 1960 Kefala moved, for the last time, to Sydney. The Sydney she arrived in that year was very different from the city I grew up in. This was the era of the White Australia policy, which had only just been relaxed to allow migration from continental Europe but continued to bar nearly everybody else. Women were still not allowed to drink in pubs. The tramways were being pulled up and expressways being built, ushering in a future of traffic jams and dodgy buses that made getting around when I was a teenager a misery. Indigenous Australians remained unrecognized in the constitution and unable to vote, and Indigenous children were still being forcibly and routinely removed from their families, a group of children known now as the Stolen Generations.

It was also the first hint of an aperture opening between Australia and the rest of the world. Kefala sailed into Sydney Harbor on a summer morning, full of light and heat and movement, its most seductive time of year. She described those first days in Sydney as something like a homecoming. "My past in Romania, in Greece, came back as a meaningful experience in a landscape that had similar resonances," she wrote. "The landscape was already feeling familiar, allowing me to survive." Survival, in many ways, equaled writing. It was only once she arrived in Sydney that Kefala became a writer.

After spending long days teaching English to other migrants, Kefala would go to the Mitchell Library and spend her evenings writing before catching the bus

INTRODUCTION

home. Her first language was Romanian, she learned French at school, and she became fluent in Greek as a teenager. Only in her twenties, in New Zealand, did she learn English, her fourth language. But when she began to write seriously, Kefala wrote in English. "I feel you have to live in a language to be able to write in it," Kefala said in a 1994 interview. "I couldn't write in Romanian or Greek or French because they were languages that I had somehow passed through. English was the language I was actually living in." But it was many years before Kefala made headway with publishers. She gradually began to suspect, from the editorial comments that *did* come back, that there was something about the issues that preoccupied her, and something about her language, which didn't quite "fit."

The Alien, Kefala's first volume of poetry, was released in 1973 by Makar Press, a small publisher that had sprung out of a student magazine at the University of Queensland. Although it was her first big break, her style was so different to what amounted to the (admittedly tiny) poetry mainstream in 1970s Australia that there were internal debates among the editors about whether it should be published at all.

To an outsider, it might seem peculiar the way that Australia's literary establishment expends time arbitrating how "Australian" or "un-Australian" a work of art is deemed to be. The US and the UK are united as the Anglophone centers of the world—around which all the other Englishes orbit, and against which the rest of us attempt to stake our territory.

Antigone Kefala's work was always fighting to find critical recognition within the boundaries of that small territory, and frequently wound up on its edges. So many contemporaneous reviews and interviews belabored questions of identity, migration, and "multiculturalism," and questioned where Kefala "fit" in the Australian literary landscape, without really ever talking about Kefala and her work itself.

When I did finally track down an Antigone Kefala book it was many years after I'd left Sydney and moved to New York. In America, I found that being Australian had become a part of my identity in a way it hadn't been at home, simply because it was now the adjective I heard most frequently used to describe myself. I was beginning to write seriously, and trying to figure out where I might fit in a national tradition. I read more Australian literature in my first years in America than I ever had before.

That was the quest I was on when I found *The Island*, on an infrequent trip home in 2018—out of print, in the Australian section of Sappho Books on Glebe Point Road, siloed off from the other fiction. I read it quickly, in the unsettling and familiar humidity of the guest room that had once been my childhood bedroom. After that, I made my way through everything I could get—Kefala's poetry, her *Sydney Journals* and *Late Journals*, and the novellas collected in *Summer Visit*.

The Island, originally published in 1984, was one of Kefala's first works of prose. A review in *The Sydney Morning Herald* used what would become familiar adjectives

v

INTRODUCTION

to describe Kefala's work: *haunting, cool, dense, impressionistic.* Another review, in *Outrider*, described *The Island* as having a "European sensibility." All of these descriptors were true, and yet none of it got at the complexity that made *The Island* so resonant and so beautiful.

The Island isn't confessional, but its autobiographical underpinnings are clear. Its protagonist, Melina, is a young university student living sometime in the mid-twentieth century, a migrant by way of Romania and Greece, and coming now into her independence. The plot is light, not really the point; the writing is most interested in the process of "becoming," trying to find a new kind of form in which the experience of being alive will crystallize. Kefala's writing is always processing the present through the past, her protagonist's experience of the present necessarily strung through and in reference to Greece, Romania, New Zealand, because how could it not be? This movement between an intensely imagined nostalgic past and the hyperreality of the present is what constitutes the hypnotic quality of *The Island*.

When *The Island* was published, Australian literature was dominated by the big, blustery novels of mostly male writers like Peter Carey and Tim Winton. Writers were beginning to reckon with the genocidal reality of Australia's colonial history, and the books that got the most attention were the ones that lent themselves best to being included on high school curricula. Something like *The Island* was radically different. On that humid afternoon when I first read *The Island* I was struck by the self-contained language, the intensely visual quali-

VI

ty of the prose, the fluidity with which Kefala moves between memories and Melina's present day, as if the border between the two were indistinct. It reminded me of other novels I had taken to calling "thin works of twentieth-century womanhood" that I was reading around that same time, books by Marina Tsvetaeva, Clarice Lispector, Marguerite Duras, Nathalie Sarraute, Christa Wolf. Each of these books struck me with the sense that I had discovered a long-lost great aunt I closely resembled.

When I reread Kefala now, it's precisely that quality of transnationality I find most poignant. I too have become somebody whose experience of the present tense is colored by my relationship to the many places I have lived in: I bicycle through Berlin behind a girl in Doc Martens and she merges with my sister in Melbourne, I drive across the Central Tablelands of New South Wales babbling to my husband about how everything reminds me of Southern California, the claustrophobia I feel in New York after an August storm reminds me that my body still expects the "cool change" of a Sydney February. This is what it is like to live along the edges, in the in-between spaces, of different countries, cultures, languages.

During the 2000s Kefala's work began to be published by Sydney's Giramondo Publishing, the champions of Australian authors who have experienced late-career revivals in America, including Gerald Murnane and Alexis Wright. When Kefala died in 2022, I learned of her passing from a eulogy sent out by Giramondo.

INTRODUCTION

Only a few weeks earlier, she had received the Patrick White Literary Award, given to a writer whose life's work has made a significant contribution to Australian literature without being adequately recognized. Now, three years later, *The Island* gets a new lease on life in this edition from Transit. I only wish it had come sooner. There are still far too few of us who whisper Kefala's name among ourselves, as a "preeminent poet from Sydney."

The copy of *The Island* sitting beside me as I write is the same one that I bought in 2018. A sticker inside attests that it was originally bought at the Feminist Bookshop in Lilyfield in 1984. It smells like Sydney. By which I mean it smells like my mother's makeup-stained sewing box in the mildewy cupboard, like the yellow photo albums lined up in my grandparents' bookshelves below the VHS tapes, it smells like the humidity of that childhood bedroom. It smells as though the elements of Sydney—saltwater, southerly winds, rotting fig and jacaranda blossoms, eucalyptus leaves baking on sandstone soil, roast lamb, Vegemite toast, passion fruit vines, magpies and cockatoos and lorikeets—all of it—had been absorbed by the glue and ink and paper. Because at the end of the day, it was Sydney that defined Antigone Kefala's work, and it was there she came to rest after decades of wandering. My copy has traveled three different continents, and two of the world's oceans, to sit here on my desk. But when I fan the pages from right to left, this book is the closest to home I could possibly be.

—*Madeleine Watts*

THE ISLAND

PART I

The office building was four stories high with narrow windows. The façade decorated with flowers and garlands that hung over each window in a plaster that had become brown with time. Inside it was full of small rooms and corridors all painted light green and smelling of disinfectant—a smell of chlorine that had permeated the whole building over the years, that had become by now second nature. Even the books, in that windowless room in which I worked, had been tinged by it.

Erik Gosse, the boss, was a myopic young man, with wild curly hair. In the morning, I could hear him open the door of his office, cut the air swiftly with the flaps of his black coat, which he seemed to wear permanently, then burst in through the door of the office, lighted by neon lights and so narrow that three people could hardly stand in the middle.

THE ISLAND

After closing the door carefully, he would remain undecided in front of the spare table, then push the papers aside and sit there dangling his legs, take out of his pockets tins of tobacco and a few pipes, and fill them greedily, his fine gold-rimmed glasses falling over his nose while he talked. And I stayed at my table pretending that I was working, listening peacefully to all that blonde noise that came in waves together with the scent of tobacco, and made no moves that could possibly alarm him. But he was more resilient than he looked, having survived in that department for so long, hiding behind a series of little mannerisms, a myopic way of looking through them, as if unaware of their existence, given to noisy outbursts which he found they would never dare interrupt.

He was doing research at the time for a book on the people who had come to the Island, in mythical times, in the big canoes, and was just discovering the tales of the "Great Woman of the Night," and the "Wingless Bird." He spoke of his theory with which he was trying to revolutionise the attitude of the country to its past. He claimed that in order to understand history, one needed a type of vision that only people placed at the crossroads could provide. That is, people who lived between cultures, who were forced to live double lives, belonging to no group, and these he called "the people in between." This vision, he maintained, was necessary to the alchemy of cultural understanding.

It was a limited hypothesis, he agreed, useful maybe only in a country such as this, in which only now were they beginning to take an interest in their past. But not quite yet, so obsessed was everyone with the future, bringing up their children as if nothing had gone before them, so that they ate and imagined that no one had eaten before them, and they built houses as if no one had built before them. Each generation that began here lived fanatically with the idea that it marked the start of the road.

As regards the past, he said, it was kept, as I could see, in all these grey metal cabinets that filled the room and had gone mouldy now, and no one talked about it in their everyday lives. It was a substance that was being examined in a few offices and universities, a secret vice, practised like taxidermy, the products of which were shown to children on holidays. And it remained in them together with the smell of antiseptic, of dust, of a decomposition that took place under glass, surrounded by artificial lights and sawdust.

He was trying his hypothesis out on me to see my reaction. I was one of those people in between. But did I have the vision? I took the idea home to discuss it with Aunt Niki and Mina over dinner. Maybe Aunt Niki had it, she was older and had been here longer. But I was still a revolutionary. I wanted other people to understand me. I wanted them all to understand me, to like me, to admire me.

I wanted us all to do marvellous things. What? I had as yet no precise idea. Some fantastic, world shattering act. I rushed forward to give them all the gifts I had, feeling always that I was not giving enough. I was full of longing for unknown things—for open spaces, warm

THE ISLAND

people, the scent of hot stones in the sun. A longing for something that would raise us, as in Byzantine paintings, make us float through the air, disappear in shafts of light, become a line in space. I was sure that there were others who felt the same. I kept watching them attentively to discern the signs.

I watched them now as I went to work, the office my first holiday job, this other side of everyday life that I had not been directly involved in before. All these morning and afternoon teas, and the lunches. Time had been divided into two categories—work and leisure. The concepts came up frequently in discussions, over lunches in the cafeteria with the formica tables and the green lavatory tiles on the walls, where they sat segregated, the women together and the men together. The men still discussing the intricacies of such concepts as "Officers and Gentlemen." Work and leisure as two separate things, with rituals that were not to be confused.

Work was an uninteresting but necessary thing, like a bitter medicine that one had to take in as small doses as possible between set given hours, say, eight o'clock in the morning and five o'clock in the afternoon. This was the sacred time of work. They all moved towards it in small faithful steps, in spite of the continuous rain, and the hail, and the wind, with neat umbrellas and plastic raincoats, and lunch boxes and an apple. Armies of them, obedient and resigned.

At five o'clock they all poured out of the doors and hurried to the leisure houses, the imposing mausoleums, built long ago, with stained glass windows and doors, and murals showing red, giant hands holding mugs from which the nectar flowed in a golden foam.

Behind the polished wooden counters, against a background of suspended, amber-coloured exotic glass fruit, the priestesses watched, those sphinx-like creatures with heavy coloured eyelids that one would glimpse when the secret doors opened for a moment as one walked down the street. They seemed to move with stylised gestures behind the altar, measuring the potions. The only women allowed into the sanctum. And each man drank as much as he could, for the doors of the leisure houses were rigidly controlled and they closed on the hour.

At six everyone hurried underground and the streets were empty. I left the office after that. I liked the empty city and went down deserted streets full of closed shops, locked buildings, lonely coffee shops that stayed open here and there. I was alone but for a few drunks, vulnerable creatures lingering in the late afternoon light searching the rubbish bins. And then there was the one I met on the post office steps. A tall, handsome man, slightly unsteady on his feet, who asked me to strike a match for him as his hands were shaking, and when he lit his cigarette he drew deeply as if inhaling a life-giving drug. His eyes dark, burning with a low muffled heat in his thin face.

"Could I walk with you for a while?" he asked.

So we went down together, the streets abandoned and desolate, full of indifferent, distant office blocks. A light wind was blowing as we approached the park, the statue of the queen rising solid in its bronze splendour.

THE ISLAND

He helped me cross the street. His eyes running lingeringly over my face, my hair. He spoke to me in fragile tones as if not to break me with the brute force of his admiration. Then he stopped suddenly as we reached the square, to examine my face. A warm feeling came out of him, warm and vulnerable; his cheeks were cavernous and his long neck thin, with an enormous Adam's apple, and his breath smelt of beer.

"Have you noticed," he asked while he searched my eyes, "have you noticed their eyes? So blue. So dead. As if nothing moves in them. And their skins, as if made of lime."

"It was the fault of the detergents," he was sure, of which they seemed so fond. The whole country was fond. Things that washed things cleaner than clean. Something wrong with their logic, he felt. What would be cleaner than clean? Yes, it must have been the detergents with which they washed their skins, their eyes, and even their eyelashes. Why they were so bent on whitewashing everything he did not know. Even the crows had been bleached. He had seen some which were half grey, half black. But the crows, he was sure, were resisting this madness of cleaning, resisting in deference to the past.

On Fridays, we went to have coffee with Erik and one of his friends, a young man that belonged to the mythical race that he was trying to write about. A short young man with a heavy skull and deep-set eyes that moved in dark, secret waters. His mouth had been cut in stone centuries earlier, and when he spoke the air filled with greenstone, a strange quality of greenstone that smelt of earth and lyre birds.

His ancestors, he said, had come from the "First Great Nothing," and he referred to his relatives as "his bones." We were very similar in this, I was telling Aunt Niki. But they considered their perspective, their individual perspective, as "magic," running through one's veins, blowing through one's nose, coming out of one's eyes, passing into everything on which a person sat, or touched, indeed perhaps on everything on which its shadow fell. To steal one's perspective was to kill the person. After one talked to him the world became full of the potential, dangerous magic of all the personalities around, and the ones that had gone before. But however dangerous it was, he talked of the past as of something immediate to him, that belonged to him, to his family, to his parents, to the great grandmother he spoke about who smoked a pipe and who had left stories of mountains crying softly in the early morning mist.

In this he resembled us, and all the people in the narrow colony we seemed to move in, all transplanted people who talked constantly of the past, that dashing figure with hot blood in its veins, and a warm skin, always rushing into some adventure, wearing colourful costumes embroidered with gold, plumed hats, flamboyant cloaks, and riding magnificent horses which later transformed into bronze and filled the squares and the parks and the gardens at home, which we could remember too. A past that was given to us children with the air and the seasons, as an everyday diet, till it became a sort of breath that moulded us and which we could no longer escape. And we began to talk of it as ours, unsure at the same time, while we performed the rituals, trying to place ourselves in a stream of time in which everything had meaning, hoping that we would suddenly acquire a value and a weight that nothing around was capable of giving us.

It was a beautiful morning. Fresh, with a perfect blue sky, deep and tight, stretched across the dome of the horizon. The path and the little bridge waited wisely between the heavy green of the trees, a rich plumage breathing unheard in the morning silence, the leaves transparent in the light.

Saturday morning, everyone was going shopping. At the bus stop, the little boy, with his plump mother and his thin father, came to sit on the bench and looked at me as if he had discovered a brilliant flower, or some bird that he admired with fascination. And he edged himself up the bench shyly, keeping his eyes constantly on me, lest I disappear. I said "Hello," and his eyes, open brown buttons, kept staring at me, unblinking.

I felt lighthearted, absurdly happy. The marvels of working, having some money, buying presents for Mother, Father, Aunt Niki, myself . . . As we stopped at the traffic lights past the swimming pool electric blue in the distance, a band was playing on the usually empty stand. All dressed in green . . . I think of Jeannie with the light brown hair . . . the music mixed with the cries of children fishing in the pond, one walking through the water holding a butterfly net in his hand.

Through the open window the coolness of the morning still lingered on the heat like a sharp exhilarating scent, the scent of the early mornings at Salt Lake. Summer. Travelling with Mother to the spa. Lumbering in the tram through the open fields, flat, stretching on both sides of the lines, and then the woods, the light rustling in the trees and, at the turn, the lake and the baths lying in the distance nestling in a hollow pocket in a bluish haze. The high wooden gates would close heavily behind us, ushering us into a dark, wet, musty antechamber, a complex of small bridges, overhanging walls, shower rooms, and through a low door we entered the baths. The cabins of raw wood, dull grey with time and full of dry, white cracks.

We took our clothes off, one by one, still warm with the heat of the body, left them to lie helpless on the bench. The boards cold, slightly wet, a brilliant wet green film covering the corners. Then we came out ashamed for a moment of our nakedness. I holding onto the well-known rails as if they were my salvation. To go and search the place for casual summer friends and explore together the cabins that were still empty. The sun was rising behind them and the light forced itself through the slight cracks and burnt in a narrow blade, solid like running water. I tried to stop it with my palm. It cut in a round golden circle, pressing against my skin with all its might, drilling to the bones.

THE ISLAND

Slowly the place filled with people, the planks hot, the lake lying still, dull grey as if made of lead, but finally, as we knew all along, we had to go through the ritual. I stood near the large wooden vat tightening all my muscles, preparing for the first sensation of mud on my skin. Mother, black already, would dip her hand into the vat and deftly rub the black shiny cream over my arms, legs, body, up to the neck. Each piece of white skin would be eaten up and then I was free to go, and watch others being dragged crying into the middle of the platform, near the vat that held the mud which sparkled in the strong light, black, like the wet skin of a sea animal, exuding a smell of sulphur, surrounded by a mass of black bodies that watched the ceremony amused, their eyes gleaming in their black faces. Sometimes, walking from one end of the baths to the other, I felt I was in a hot underworld surrounded by a new race of people.

At midday the place was full. We left then and travelled home, the wind blowing hot across the fields, my skin stretched tight, a tiredness rising out of me, the trees flowing gaily, everything shimmering in the heat. We would go home, to the cool house, the curtains drawn, to have lunch, the place full of contentment and peace . . .

When I came back from shopping, Aunt Niki and Mina were having coffee on the verandah and reading the papers. From the street a car would pass swiftly, and then the silence folded again, falling softly over the trees, cat stretched out in the shade of the bushes. On the chimney of the doctor's house a large, grey-white bird was resting. The sky blue-silver, like pearls, and the bird still as a statue for a time, the curve of its breast watching the horizon, a perfect view from up there, then turning on all sides to watch the perspective, and from afar, the sound of birds crying in an unknown dialect to which she seemed to be listening carefully while scratching her ear, or putting her head in her breast feathers with a dislocated grace.

Summer! Summer! If only it would last. I smelt the sun on my skin. —Aunt Niki, did you go to the Salt Lake? She looked up startled. Began to laugh. —The things that you remember. Yes, we used to go with Mother, before I got married. Much before your time.

I could never imagine Aunt Niki at home, although I knew that she had lived there. Her image belonged to photographs, this glamorous, elegant creature in close-fitted hats and fur coats, like Greta Garbo, smiling under the winter trees in the Tuileries Gardens, who sent postcards from Egypt—red-orange exotic sunsets, and indigo-blue summer nights with the black massive shape of the Sphinx in the distance.

I stayed in the sun under my straw hat listening to the rustling of the papers, feeling full of light, rising out of the valley with the warm air, flowing above the evergreen grass and the trees, higher and higher.

I always had such a feeling of release when the train moved out of the station, as if going towards adventures, great journeys, a feeling that did not last past the suburbs.

THE ISLAND

As the train came out of the tunnel on the other side, and turned, the city faced us, just as I remembered it that first evening from the boat. This large soft animal resting its flanks on the marble surface of the sea. The lights on the small hills sparkling through the blue-violet air. A deep silence enveloping the harbour and the waters, deeper and deeper cushioned by the fine needles of rain that were falling.

Then we went on as if riding an enormous caterpillar, banging and clanging along the rails like a dark beast pushed forward by heavy heartaches in the night. Unsure somehow, unsettled, changing direction every second, then stopping with the clutter of its hundred iron limbs, coming to rest with a heavy sigh in the middle of the empty countryside. Voices would ring out in meaningless tongues, and then we would start again horsewhipped in another direction.

I walked along the seafront towards the house that waited like a lighted frame at the top of the dark hill. The moon was on the waters, lighting white patches around the heavy islands somewhere. A distant country in which the moon dominated silently, and from where the dark waves travelled unceasingly, like hands touching the sand with a rustle of silk.

"How long can we live?" Mother was saying. "You must find yourself someone not to be alone." The nights were so black. She dreamt of people coming and going all the time, above the sound of the wind and the rain. Every night she seemed to return home, walk in the old streets, meet acquaintances to whom she explained that we now lived in this faraway country. Our street unchanged, full of the same acacia trees, the garden overgrown with weeds, and as she opened the front door, the house would wait empty, the wallpaper showing the marks of the frames that had been removed, the curtains drawn, an anaemic light coming through them, the carpets dusty and threadbare. She always woke up full of this agonised fear—how was she going to come back to us.

Over dinner they talked again of home. All the porcelain and glass, gone now, and Grandmother's silver candelabras, all that furniture that had belonged to so many generations, all neatly set out in the dowry document, duly signed by everyone. Walnut tables, like a magic incantation, rosewood bedrooms in the Street of Roses. The heavy brocade curtains and Grandmother in bed, listening, to hear if anyone, a thief, opened her special wardrobe where she kept her jewels. Intimate bedrooms where they would put me to sleep and of which I remembered nothing, except that Grandmother still insisted on using lamps, the light through the translucent angel's-tears–pink glass, and the little fir tree cut in crystal. My only memory was of lying in bed on the enormous feather pillows, half-closing my eyes, catching on the end of my eyelashes the flames that went through the tree, breaking them into geometrical shapes, red, violet, gleaming blue, small scintillating planets turning around the orbit of my eyes, till the tree became a tall white candle burning in the room.

All the exciting things had happened before I was born, or when I was too little to remember. The war

THE ISLAND

came when you were born, they all said. All the inter-
esting people had gone too, my Great-Aunt Garyfalo,
for instance, whom I was supposed to resemble. A tall,
handsome woman in the photographs, very proud and
strong-willed. The past, as Mother said, here to torture
us all the time.

I went to have a bath. I imagined that I could put
everything right with a bath. Then I became aware of
the music. The darkness had descended on everything
and it was twelve o'clock. The house opposite was full
of lights, the curtains were drawn, the windows were
opened, and the music rushed out in powerful sounds
reverberating everywhere. Cruel, metallic sounds that
went on rocking the night, as if the sky was an amplified
chamber beating with electricity. And the voices went
on droning in the background, repetitive mouths that
made steel noises that went on and on unbearably.

I went to bed and began to think of all the beds that
I had slept in, all the noises that had not let me sleep, in
the streets, in houses, the bones of the old lift rattling like
a ghost, puffing up the shaft. In closed suffocating places,
the breaths of people stale and tired filling the air, and all
the women that went down the corridors in that large
dilapidated hotel by the sea, where we had suddenly become refugees. The grounds full of small tortured trees,
and beyond them the sea. The women who went down
the corridors between the broken windows nailed with
planks, full-bodied, in silk petticoats or flimsy panties
under their housecoats, arranging their hair, and a scent
of stale perfume, and the beds that I saw on my way

to school through the half-opened doors, in which they had made love to the sleepy-eyed men who marched out of the building each morning, going forward to find jobs.

I was always on the verge of some dark secret belonging to the adults, something that you were not supposed to know but guessed with instinctive accuracy. All those frightening things that love and passion brought with them, hot brutalities which I watched with fascination, both drawn and repelled by the spectacle.

I went to school, past rooms and corridors full of luggage, trunks, old women waiting long days near suitcases that seemed to multiply as if giant chickens gave them birth every night and they had to be counted anxiously every morning, with shaky hands, heads covered in black shawls, bags full of keys.

It was suffocating in there, as if in a prison, the corridors and the rooms and the grounds filled by continuous waves of refugees, mostly from up north where the new war had started. It was only in the morning that the building seemed spacious. The cleaners had already been at work, and the magnificent marble staircase was white, the veins showing through the translucent skin of the stone.

Outside, the grounds were grey, the closed chapel distant in the early sun rays, and behind it the scraggy trees looked dishevelled, like the hair of an old woman sleeping in the fields.

It was the only time I felt attached to the building, loving and detesting it in turns, trapped among all these

THE ISLAND

people, dreaming constantly of how we would escape, become again ourselves, away from all these people, so close to us, this herd which we had been forced to join. I dreamt of the time when there would be only silence and space around us.

We were back at the University, in our places in the library, the smell of old paper around us, each in his favourite spot, like a little kingdom one had fenced imaginatively and where one felt at home. Ashton, as usual, below the stained-glass window showing the awkward knights with the disproportionately large armoured feet and very small heads—obviously not intellectuals, Michael said. Opposite him Kate was reading, already hugging the radiator. She had grown her hair during the holidays and was wearing it in a bun on the crown of her head. She looked like a Rossetti painting, those permanently fragile young girls, with deep-blue eyes and perfect oval faces.

We went down with Ashton to check the arrangements for the tutorial. We knocked at the dark, heavy door, waited, then knocked again. He called from inside and we went in, closing the door behind us. The large desk in the middle of the room was neatly arranged. He was sitting pinched at the edge of the chair, his thin nose red.

I spoke. I could see from his face that he had not the faintest idea what I was saying, the meaning stopped somewhere midair between us, he incredulous that he will ever understand me, I incredulous that he will ever understand me. He was busy swallowing thin mouthfuls of vinegar, watching me with preoccupied eyes, rubbing his hands as if drying them of sand, trying to get rid of it. I could see in his whole attitude the immense surprise at being confronted, here in his own room, at the University, by something as foreign as myself. The implied extravagance of my voice, the rapid nervousness of my movements, my eyes that looked too directly at him. He made social concessions outwardly, but inwardly he kept repeating to himself—why the hell do I have to put up with this in my everyday life, one is not safe anywhere these days. The intensity of the preoccupation absorbed his concentration. He turned to Ashton for relief, Ashton who was waiting indifferent, his hands motionless.

Ashton spoke in his flat, matter-of-fact voice. Dr. Jackson replied like a man indulging in a luxury. Each sound, each word handled carefully as if it were a porcelain cup of rare origin that has been kept under glass in a household of collectors, displayed or handed around only when visitors arrived.

Totally dejected, I followed Ashton out of the room and went discouraged down the corridor, past lectures in progress, down the stairs and into the cafeteria. We stayed at the green formica tables closed in by the sandstone walls. The nature of the understatement, as I was telling Aunt Niki, was more miraculous and more subtle than the Pindaric ode, and I had already given up hope that I would ever master it.

I stayed there, with that black uninteresting liquid which they called coffee in front of me, the place full of young men with heavy jaws made of iron who could make the silence sink below any imagined level, like

THE ISLAND

Ashton, clenching and unclenching his teeth, staring vacantly before him. There was no need to get excited, his hands said, his coat, his face. He looked around at the other tables, overwhelmed by my vehemence. He had never asked for this, he told them, he was not responsible. He opened a packet of cigarettes laboriously, offered me one, and waited for the thing to pass.

It was obvious that the effort was not worth it. I was suddenly silent, the air getting rustier and rustier and so heavy that a movement became impossible to imagine— my jaws became of iron and left a bitter taste in my mouth. I wondered for a moment how I could ever find the energy to break those insurmountable mountains of resistance.

It was only at sports that the animal in them leaped out across the well-trimmed lawns, jumped and ran letting out hoarse cries, and when the game had finished they all collapsed again, trailing their iron chains across the wet corridors in the semidarkness of the stained-glass windows and into the cafeteria where they stayed at the tables mute as statues.

I felt like doing something wild. Shake them. Set them on fire. Thaw out those fine needles of ice that seemed to live permanently at the binding of their nerves. Yet nothing could be done, I knew as I watched Ashton smoking, ill at ease and tense on the other side of the table. It could not be done even on a personal basis.

Ashton, who had been there from the beginning, with his dark-brown hair, his strong face, handsome almost in certain lights, his blue-green eyes with long eyelashes that made him look very boyish.

He approached and was exhausted by the effort and, when he sat down, he seemed to want very much to be alone. His hands, strong hands, lumbered in a heavy sleep, as if they had been frostbitten in a winter a long time ago and had never regained their flexibility. He seemed permanently awkward and unloved, an orphan that needed warmth, and I felt guilty and tried to make him feel at ease. I told him stories to warm him up, stories that I had heard at home. But he was afraid. He did not know what to do. No one had prepared him. He felt uncomfortable, exposed to an intimacy of friendship he was not used to, everything too near, too personal. He shifted a little in his chair, smiled a sociable, waxy smile, frowned, and said, trying to bring everything to normal, "Yes, yes, it was quite nice, raining a little, but it wasn't too bad." He wanted unobtrusive gestures, a warmth measured in drops, small distant approvals. He felt at ease only in a world of small, distant approvals.

But maybe we were all changing without realising it, becoming like them. The other night, visiting Anna, I was listening to Mrs. Kousis, her voice falling and rising on those honeyed expressions . . . my doll . . . my golden one . . . that came so readily, so naturally in Greek, unostentatious, like an old litany that one has grown up with, unnoticed. Now she seemed to use them emptily, without enthusiasm, an old habit.

Yet here was the voice, battling on bravely as before, trying to humanise the coldness of the air, to recreate the old mirage of little cups of coffee in the afternoons, fortune-telling from the intricate patterns in the cup, ter-

THE ISLAND

races and familiar glimpses of the sea, kaikia, fig trees, but her eyes had lost the onyx-like brilliance that they had when I first met Anna at school.

In the dream I was in unknown streets trying to get rid of this rabbit (or was it a hare?). White, small, with rather bristly hair, and very warm, human eyes. I was trying desperately to get rid of it, to leave it behind me and close doors between us. I pushed it into corners, ran ahead of it, pretending that I did not know it, but everywhere I looked, there it was, sticking close to me. I could read in its eyes that it knew very well that I wanted to be rid of it, but it was patiently waiting for the mood to pass.

Then I was in a boat full of people, Dr. Jackson was there dressed in a brown tweed suit with a vest and a cape. I was offering the hare to him, but he did not want it. He was going to Europe, he said, in the same slow, indifferent voice, and could not possibly take it with him.

The animal was waiting, a few brown hairs coming out of its moustache, and then we were both running down a hill. It was running with me, good naturedly, trying to humour me . . . and then I woke up . . .

Mother was laughing, her eyes rested, glossy brown.

"It must be the essay, running after you in the dream . . ." The kitchen was warm and full of light, she was delicately arranging the half-moon cakes on the buttered dish. On the radio, someone was singing "Vissi d'arte."

Outside, the morning was charged with the cry of lawn mowers. All around the hills and down the valley, the Sunday gardeners were out in force again, cutting the grass, trimming it, shearing it, with machines, by hand, stubbornly trying to keep it to that fanatic short-haired green carpet. A consistent war was being waged, a war to the death, this desperation in their hearts not to be annihilated by grass.

Watching them all, I remembered again that first journey from the camp to the city. A cold overcast day. The country unrolled hilly and green. Now and again we would stop and, as the rain started, the stations were full of tall, heavy people in rubber boots, rolling cigarettes with rough hands, watching the train morosely from below wide-brimmed hats.

And as we travelled, the stations became smaller and smaller, as if tokens of some last human effort that hardly survived in this ocean of grass that moved like horses' manes over the distance. The land seemed to be waiting, like a silent, closed-in enemy, to take over immediately the struggle ended. Broken-down skeletons of houses, the rusty limbs of machines glimpsed before being swallowed up. The secret heart of the land seemed to be yearning for that uninterrupted silence free of humans that had been there before, the presence of that time still in the land's memory.

Later when we stopped for lunch, the road teeming with rain, we watched through the windows a tall woman in the shelter of the station carefully take off her hat, her shoes, and her stockings, store them in her basket

THE ISLAND

and then go out into the road, while the rain poured on her.

What everyone knew, and what they proclaimed everywhere, was that the material was of paramount importance and had to be saved at all costs, but the human was incidental and dispensable, and its needs were only physical. It must have been the struggle, for so many generations, to tame, to subdue this unknown land that had filled them slowly with such a narrow fanaticism for material things. Or was it the land that took its revenge slowly, wooing them with its lush richness, playing a never-ending game with their spirits, holding them and freeing them, yet possessing them, blinding their eyes, shaping them in silence till only its voice could be heard in the country, weighing them down, binding them, deeper and deeper, till they could no longer rise, till the light in them withered and they walked burdened and morose, suspicious and stubborn, talking of mending fences, killing pests, keeping cows, selling beef . . .

Down on the beach the cars were already beginning to arrive. It was drizzling now, but as the day advanced, more and more cars arrived, and people, whole families with children and grandmothers, set up house on the beach, in the sand, took out their tables and chairs and picnic baskets and forks and knives and thermoses and bottles and bottles of beer. And the wind blew sand in their drinks and their sandwiches, but they stayed there stoically, eating and drinking and talking about the weather, while the rain came down in fine needles.

In the afternoon they all packed up and went. I left too, to go back to the city. I walked along the beach, turning to wave to Mother who was watching from the front windows, feeling guilty that I was abandoning her. Everything was already shut, the houses and the tea rooms, waiting for the darkness to descend on the hills, and the sea to disappear. And in the salt-eaten wooden houses, they waited to enter that cocoon of silence and go to sleep. I walked down to the station angry and desperate. We were trapped again. There was no future here. We had no future. Who could imagine a future in this mean, cold, grass-trimmed country. I hated it. I hated the whole place, the green hills and the sheep permanently grazing the same spots, as if they had been painted there, and the wind going through you, coming at you out of corners, chilling the surface of the sea, bleached dark green like dying leaves.

And in the waiting room, the windows spotted with sea air and a stale smell of fish and chips and disinfectant, an elderly woman sitting next to me on the wooden bench, with a tea cosy for a hat, turned to remark: "The hills, so beautifully green with the rain."

Loula Alexiou had warm brown eyes with dusted eyelashes, well-shaped cheekbones and a slender body always wrapped in a bone-coloured raincoat, with a belt that she wore very tight, and which gave her the waist of an adolescent girl. She came on Sundays for lunch, sad-eyed, one hand inside the hip pocket of her raincoat, the other carrying a small bag and a book. She balanced herself gingerly on her high heels, looking like a romantic figure in a post-war French film, one of those heroines we used to watch at the Roxy picture theatre, who leaned against the lamp posts surrounded by a mist that filtered like a haze around them, their eyes full of the tragedies of war, of lost loves, lost lives, in their raincoats, collars up, forever tying and untying their belts with nervous fingers, or stubbing out their cigarettes, waiting in deserted cafes while outside the rain fell on desolate streets.

She stayed in the kitchen with Aunt Niki, beating the egg and lemon for the avgolemono soup, or cutting tomatoes, or simply staring out of the small windows into the wilderness of the garden. A garden which was seldom touched, except to clean the path and a space around the plum tree. Aunt Niki ignored it, as she ignored the house; it had nothing to do with her, a house that uncle had bought just before he died, and to which she could never get attached. She was disconnected from it, she neither presented it to people, nor did she apologise for it. It was something like a hotel that belonged to someone else and in which she lived an improvised life.

Loula watched through the windows the rain dripping from the evergreen leaves, the walls green, the wetness entering your bones. She spoke in whispers of Miki, her dead husband, and cried. Spoke of how she dreamt that he was still alive, and when she woke up in the morning she had to relive his death day by day. The way he fell on his face in the street, the faint thread of blood at the corner of his lips.

They both stayed in the kitchen and cried over her sorrows, over their sorrows, over the sorrows of the world. Touched by that "infinite disaster," as Anna Comnena has called it (a fire that lights up with torches the secret places and burns, but does not consume with burning, parching the heart imperceptibly . . . a fire that strikes the bones, the marrow, and the heart's centre . . .).

I was cleaning the house. The sharp voice of the vacuum cleaner drowned their voices, from time to time I could see Loula wiping her eyes. What could I do to save them? They were going one by one and I could do nothing to stop it. Like the telegram last month, so deceptively simple. "Buried last Sunday." The more we watched it the rock-like solidity of the words became more and more apparent. Whatever we did we could not change them, they enclosed forever an event that no amount of energy would alter. "Buried last Sunday." We moved around the event, trying to alter it somehow, to give it something of ourselves, to absorb something of it. But the event in itself would be no closer to us than in the beginning.

Mother remembered him when he was young. The debonair young man with the top hats and the silver canes, and anecdotes that could no longer hold him. I only remembered him old. The last time I had seen him it was as if he was already possessed by that unknown towards which he was moving. It was as if slowly, imperceptibly he was going towards it, and he was becoming

THE ISLAND

indifferent, more tired, careless of time, of movement, tinged. As if the sickness of eternity had already possessed him and he lived out of habit only. He was moving further and further away from the human circle, towards that neutral place where human things were meaningless. Those waves of silence that moved in the pauses between his gestures.

What could I do to save them? What miracle could I perform to help life which was being constantly decimated by everyday living, while death stayed intact, to strike suddenly with its full force. There was nothing one could do, so everyone said, except pray and cry. Cry like the black-clad woman in the bombed house near that hotel by the sea, who lighted the oil lamps in front of the icons every night, alone in that house that stood, in a neighbourhood reduced to rubble by the bombs. Lighted them every night and wept for her lost son, mourned over his lost eyes, limbs, skin that she would never see again, her only child, her gift, grown in her body day by day, taking shape, moving. Cried with a terrorising desperation, her voice flying out of the broken windows through the air as if wild geese beating their wings. Then it would subside, whimpering, wailing, insistent, like the church chants at Easter, where we were all marched with the school, sheep-like, to reenact the fable.

This cult of suffering, these nailed feet and palms, that crucified body that hung forever above our heads, in corners, in altars, below the chandeliers, burning in the candlelight, suspended forever in pain, transfixed in agony. An agony that became our responsibility, that made us guilty, pointed forever at us. So that we wore it in chains around our necks, kissed it in reverence, we shaped it with our hands, we burnt it in our minds, till we were born with it indistinguishable from our blood. A blood that was resurrected forever so that it could fall in drops, insistent, inexhaustible, as a tangible sign of our initial guilt, a sacrifice that was reenacted for centuries, never allowed to free itself.

But I did not want his sacrifice. I could not bear his sacrifice. I had no original sin. I had not fallen from Paradise. I had been born free. I wanted us all to revolt. I wanted us to fight. Why should we worship suffering forever? Why should we acquiesce?

I watched the giant candelabras, golden, rising like sunflowers full of sparkling points, and all around us in the semidarkness of the columns, from the human texture of the walls seeped in candle smoke, burnt oil, incense fumes, the faces of the saints looked at us with their mellow limpid eyes, docile and full of love. They all floated at ease in this inner agony.

And as we came out, the rocky streets stretched up towards the sky, and the skeletons of the bombed houses stood in the heat, timeless, the sockets of their windows gaping, and the light poured down, evaporated in the air, crystallised and left the particles suspended, sparkling white, radiating an energy that filled the air . . .

In the cleaned house we all sat down to lunch. Aunt Niki at the head of the table, serving herself first and then passing the dishes. We tried to make conversation, Mina telling us of the circular she had found in the letterbox, a local gardener offering his services . . . trimming trees, cutting grass, looking after roses, and finally recommending himself as "a very reliable poisoner." We all laughed. Aunt Niki said that she could use one at the office.

Loula watched us unseeing, her ever-silent face and eyes unmoved, untouched by anything around her. The delicate hue of her skin the colour of old marble. She seemed tired, her eyes bulging out of that small bony face as in those photographs of starved, tortured children that could be seen everywhere after the war, children who had accumulated a knowledge reserved in other times for adults, a knowledge that was too heavy for them to carry. Aunt Niki sat at the head of the table, her eyes preoccupied, handsome eyes, like two lights that carried the head and the large generous mouth. Inside her a sort of backbone held her up, with a slight suggestion of stiffness.

"This inability I seem to suffer from," Loula was saying, "to familiarise myself with my life's happenings."

After she had gone, we washed the dishes with Aunt Niki. It was getting dark and the lady opossum had arrived, standing on the barrel with her children, eating bread daintily with her front paws and watching us fascinated through the window.

"The much more dreadful truth about everything," Aunt Niki was saying, "is that nothing lasts. Except the repetitiousness of things. Look at myself. Six years have gone since Iorgo died, and I am still here. Cooking in the same kitchen, drinking out of the same cups. Yes, this is the terrible truth—nothing lasts. When Mother was dying, I felt that my love for Iorgo was like a tree, a tree I was carrying inside, an immense powerful tree that filled my body, the roots, the branches were everywhere, in my lungs, in my stomach, in my flesh, fine, powerful, invisible things holding the soil inside, giving it shape. It was as if inside I was full of this warm, reassuring weight, yet light, but so deeply a part of me that it was impossible to distinguish them from my own nerves, veins. And I was sure that if something were to happen to him, it would destroy me too . . ."

The fear of their deaths was a permanent feeling in me, rehearsed since childhood. The first time that Mother went away without us, I dreamt every night that I was walking down avenues of cemeteries always covered in warm apricot-coloured gravel, silent walls of cypress trees on either side. I small, very small, seeing myself from the back, as well as being the main actor. Led by the hand by a man, always unknown, past mausoleums of brilliant stained glass, cobalt blues and golds, to be led to an open grave that was Mother's. Afraid to look inside. Crying. Always awake at this point.

It was summer, and the moon was pouring in my room, enveloping everything in a sharp white blueness. I was shrouded in blue, and the heavy scent of the petunias and the queen of the nights drifted in through the curtains.

PART II

They were dancing on the stage, tall doll-like girls in starched elaborate headgear and embroidered aprons, raising clouds of dust. How long did we have to wait till our turn came? I tried not to think of it. Alexi would no doubt tell us. My stomach felt hollow. They were on the other side of the stage calling me, the curtain had come down and in the middle of the stage the small, exotic-looking adolescent was preparing. His body was covered in rich brocade, deep golden yellows and blues, layers of flamboyant feathers, his small exquisite feet naked. His hands wore enormously long painted nails.

And as the curtain rose, a chant-like melody filled the air, plaintive, all the endless desolation of the desert at midday transformed into a thin metallic sound that stretched undulating with an unobtrusive insistence. In the dry emptiness of the stage the bird stamped the ground gravely, moved its plumage, its rich wings, in slow sweeping curves. It measured the enemy, touching the ground with its beak, froze in silence ready to attack, and in the bell-like sounds that filled the air, jumped again and again, its golden feathers circles of colour in the air.

"Melina, our turn."

We arranged ourselves in a hurry.

"Don't worry," said Alexi, "I shall give you the entrance and the right note." The limelight blinded me for a moment as the curtain rose. When I looked up, the stream of light from above broke on my eyelids, and as far as I could see, over the darkness of their heads and the columns, there was only a nebulous white sun that turned and advanced making my eyelids sparkle. We were already past our first songs, into my solo part, Alexi tracing the imaginary tempo. But I was no longer aware of their voices, only of the velvety darkness of the theatre, the brilliant sun, and my voice, singing independently of me now, resonant, caressing their faces, the voice that went on alone, possessed with its own tempo, riding the air.

Past the applause, the curtain came down slowly, and as we moved to the wings, Dinos came to embrace me, kiss me on both cheeks. "Between artists," he said and laughed. Alexi was in a corner watching with serious eyes.

We left through dark corridors and fire escapes. The streets were empty, violet blue, as if the air had been painted, sprayed with particles of colour. I walked with the others in silence, warm still. We went down the ramp into Claridges, the new coffee shop. The artificial fountain rose in the middle, full of phosphorescent coloured lights. For a moment we seemed lost in a dark underworld of candles and mask-like faces with gleaming eyes. We sat down, past the aquarium in which red fish travelled listlessly in the green liquid.

Dinos bent across the table at the same time as Alexi, both offering me a rose. We all laughed.

"Nothing for me?" Anna said, and took Alexi's rose.

We had seen each other quite often over the last few weeks because of the "International Concert," as Aunt Niki ironically called it. I liked Alexi. He was the unknown. One half guessed, in the deft quickness of his reactions, his dark silences, a secretive force inside him that made him alive. He moved with the stylised grace of an animal of good breed. But Anna liked him, loved him, claimed him. It was difficult to see if he were aware of this—her possession. Dinos had chosen me, on the surface, but it was all a game, a game that would not last, now that the concert was over. We would go back into our own worlds, I to the University, Anna to the office. Alexi and Dinos worked together, trained architects at home, but working here as draughtsmen.

But tonight we were at ease with each other, there was a bond between us, people who had faced a common enemy together. We were full of stories and we laughed and filled the air with extravagant gestures and sounds to impress the subdued, uninteresting people around us. Everything was slightly unreal tonight.

When I came out of the bus, a wet misty darkness was falling, and on top of the hill, the houses crouched

THE ISLAND

against each other, their eyes burning. Witches, as Mina said.

One could imagine that they had come out of a story by Gogol, the two burning eyes, yellow, and were riding on top of the hill against the night sky, dark like charcoal.

The pine tree rustled as I came down the steep hill, and, under the bridge, the water rushed through the leaves of the fallen limbs of the tree. The deeper I went deeper was the silence, as if the valley had no resonance.

Aunt Niki was still up, playing her patience on the dining room table.

"Ah!" Her eyes lighted up. "I thought you will never come. I was waiting to hear how it went."

I went into the kitchen to make coffee, excitedly calling out snippets of information. An old habit that had persisted through the years. The beginnings were lost somewhere at home. I could see myself in the school uniform following mother everywhere, in and out of the rooms, in the garden, flooding her in an avalanche of words, describing everything that I had seen, people, places, events. Then and now out of the same need, to make them all participate, to give them all my eyes, my touch, my smell, so that between us there would be no unknown ground standing in the way. A constant feeling of guilt that I was full of riches from which others had been excluded.

Now, in the lighted room, Aunt Niki filling the air with puffs of smoke, trying to find the right card for her patience, I launched enthusiastically, for I loved to talk, and Aunt Niki liked me, admired me as something out of the ordinary, as if she recognised in me things that she considered of value, giving me scope to do things and say things that she would not give to others. I felt at home with her, yet sometimes with a slight, but very slight, foreignness towards myself, so that as I talked I watched myself from the corner of my eye to see if the finishing touches were aesthetic enough. For Aunt Niki loved decorum, the living decorum of one's life that must be kept always cultivated, polished, so that one could move gracefully among centuries of stylised gestures.

At the end of the corridor, through the glass doors, the tall lanky man in the white shirt and the black trousers, the red sash at his waist, stood behind the espresso coffee machine pulling the levers down. The air smelt of coffee.

I went up the hollow stairs, bare and dry. At the second turning was the open door of the gallery.

There was no one in. Only the white spaciousness of the drawings, and the stark black lines that had captured the essentials in two strokes. The bulldog, heavy, powerful face of the writer, the child's legs, sturdy, caught moving on the cobblestones in the sun. The more I watched them the livelier they became, as if all the legs I had seen were never legs, none of them had the essential leg quality of these two. Here they were running in the sun, unconcerned with anything but walking.

THE ISLAND

Someone put an arm around my shoulders and when I turned, there was Dinos.

"You here too?"

"I, of course, professional interest."

I was annoyed, annoyed that I had been interrupted, but Alexi was there, smiling.

"They are fantastic, aren't they?" he said.

I turned towards him eagerly, ignoring Dinos, punishing him for interrupting me, for his possessive attitude.

We went round the gallery together, slowly. I, too preoccupied now to notice anything, too involved with his face, his skin, his clothes, his entire being. I felt excited and afraid, my skin seemed alive, and my eyes, my voice came resonant from the depths of my throat with a glow that changed his eyes, made them intense and glossy, made him look at me as if at something infinitely rare, precious, something that he was discovering for the first time, staggered by the discovery. And I bent my head, moved my fingers through the air, with Aunt Garyfalo's gold ring, turned to see Dinos following obstinately and laughed out of an unsuspected happiness. Alexi was mine, all mine, I knew it. I could see it in his face, in his eyes, abandoning for a moment his will, offering it to me totally . . . This frightened me suddenly. As I reached the door I had only one thought, how to escape. I made some unintelligible excuse and flew out, leaving him in the middle of the white, shiny gallery, conquered and lost.

I ran down the stairs, my heart beating, regretting already that I had left. Someone was following. But as I reached the corridor Dinos was calling.

We went out and walked down the empty streets. The air waited and the pavements too. Six o'clock. The shops were closed, everybody had gone home. Home for a cup of tea. I knew that he was feeling slightly out of place but I was not going to help him. Then, as usual, his anger turned against these foreign streets, these small ugly shops, the narrowness of life he found everywhere, the six o'clock closing . . . I knew all the arguments by heart, I was already beyond them in that form.

I followed his suede shoes and the dark grey trousers that shaped his lean legs. Someone had asked me the other day, "Who was that tall, handsome man I saw you with?" Yes, he was proud of his body, he had the greatest respect for it and an implicit belief in the supremacy of its needs. He was proud of any physical achievement and disdained intellectual fireworks, yet considered himself a good talker. Or maybe he talked, as I did, to cover the distance between us.

He talked a lot, told jokes about friends, football games, life at the University, afraid somehow of my silence. And I could not decide whether I liked him or whether I was only flattered by his attention. But with him my ability to evaluate, to feel reactions by small imperceptible signs, to move with ease in a social environment, had returned. I felt on familiar ground. I could approximate his past, I felt that we came from the same world, a world that had given us at birth, and later, through impalpable ways, through the sun, the air, a cer-

THE ISLAND

tain type of antennae, formed us to feel the texture of a human being, of a situation, of a move, by unexpressed ways, a core of undefined perception that went deeper than customs or language to the very roots of a soil.

The bus was coming. I turned to say good-bye.

"When am I going to see you?"

"Ring," I said, turning to face the staring faces in the bus.

The Vegetarian Restaurant was full of people in wind jackets, clipped trouser legs, heavy boots. People who had come far away, through arctic regions, still blown by the strong winds, and who were eating, dishevelled, concentrating on their hot soups. The walls were full of pictures of lakes and flowers, discoloured now, and in all the corners faded plastic flowers rose stiffly out of the large, embossed verdigris brass vases.

We stayed in our coats drinking mint tea and eating pumpkin cake. The wails of a baby reached from the second dining room, sharp and desolate, floating above the chipped crockery and the smell of fried onions, and the heavy forks and knives and spoons, lying wearily on the table, weighed down with time and tiredness, as if they could never imagine a movement, the spring of their functional days gone forever.

We were on our way to a rehearsal at the French Club, a students' show, called *Love Through the Ages*. We were playing a scene from *Andromaque*. I was Andromaque, and Ashton, the King, madly in love with me. I had to be aloof, sad, still obsessed by the memory of my dead husband, Hector . . .

Andromaque, je pense à vous! Ce petit fleuve,
Pauvre et triste miroir où jadis resplendit
L'immense majesté de vos douleurs de veuve . . .

I was quoting Baudelaire to myself. To make a point with Ashton one had to quote Hardy, who had gripped him recently. He had already read most of his novels and was now going through his poetry, biographies—a world with which he felt some affinity.

Just then, the red curtain drawn across the door to stop the wind opened slightly, unobtrusively, and through the narrow gap a tall, lanky figure poured slowly inside, trying to gather together his long legs covered in bright-blue jeans. He waited for a second looking around, then, as if recognising Ashton, moved with a false modesty towards our table, bending his legs at the knees, as if they were made of wood. I wondered if he were not cold, he had only a light blue jumper on, of the same ridiculous baby colour as the jeans, which stretched across his wide stomach and flat chest, and out of the short sleeves his hairy arms hung heavy like round hunks of wood, covered in freckles and ending in large hands—they must have weighed tons.

"May I?"

Ashton nodded, cleared his throat, turned to introduce him: "Max Newman—Melina Pappa."

THE ISLAND

He smiled, his glassy eyes reaching full of a false virginal shyness from under his overgrown eyebrows.

"How nice to find you here, and with Melina too." He used my first name immediately, and I was annoyed. He went on to discuss the Bushwalkers Club, where they had apparently met. He pursed his lips like a young child, well brought up, who has been told that the soup must be sipped slowly and silently.

"Are you a member?" he asked me.

The tone was submissive and apologetic, but the voice strangely masculine, powerful, reaching from the depths of a well through layers of darkness. It was so out of touch with the rest of him that it seemed indecent.

"No," I said laughing, "I am allergic to sport."

"Oh, but you must," he became more animated now, "walking is not a sport . . ."

The skin of his face was hardened like hide and his nose bright red as if he had worked in the fields. But his face had no expression at all, only a virginal smile that came out now and again between vegetarianism and peace councils, and his hate of violence, and his Indian gurus. This and a medicinal smell that seemed to emanate from his baby-blue jumper, in between confessions of an undecided future, looking for a partner, and a desire to find a way and a salvation. When we got up to go, he bent down and kissed my hands, held them in his for a while, as if warming himself.

"Sorry about that," Ashton said as we were going down the stairs.

When we came out it was bitterly cold. The rain had

stopped. It was lunchtime. The narrow streets were full of people eating fish and chips, pies, watching the shop windows. One had the impression that the entire country had been starving, and now they had all invaded the streets and were attacking food full of ardour and determination. Boiled peas and butter, roasted leg of lamb, and chickens, perfectly roasted plexiglass chickens, eternally turning under the electric lights.

The stage was full of nineteenth-century people dressed in long crinoline dresses and shawls, men with big cravats and vests and short boots with buttons. Their faces painted like masks, dead white with oval black eyes crossed by a line. They moved expressionless through all the tortures of family life. Then the two of them were left alone. The man in his buttoned boots, his check trousers and white vest, with pale lips and uncertain movements and a nervously twitching mouth, and his bride, with three noses, covered in flowing robes, transparent veils of the most refined spiderwebs. Both bathing in a green underwater light, she calm as if floating on the surface of waters, indifferent yet passionate.

She spun round and round out of the green light, webs that changed in depth and transparency, now becoming blue, sapphire blue, like waters breaking on a deserted beach, in a strong summer light, their sound deafening, and now emerald green, quiet and still, glasslike around the man, till he slowly became less and less nervous, less and less unwilling, more and more pliant, struggling at times here and there but unsuccessfully against this magic of green that kept us all spellbound and breathless. Till we also wished to be submerged in this peaceful element, where there were no problems, no troubles, but only a deep, glass-like silence, a deep engulfing silence all around, through which we would watch life with mask-like faces and black burning eyes.

When we left we were all silent. We walked in groups down the bare streets in the moonlight. Ashton walked by my side clenching and unclenching his teeth, and Dinos's laugh exploded in the night against the closed walls.

The house was large, white, with an ascetic, monastic air about it. Big, half-empty rooms, fur rugs on the floor as we passed the wide arched hall greeted by Guy Nemours—still in his buttoned-up boots, and his white vest, with black mobile eyes. His wife, blonde, plump, with an indolent sensuality about her.

The rooms were hot, the entire house stood still, waiting for us to come, fires burning in its fireplaces, food spread on little tables, drinks. After a while the noise subsided and the floor cleared for dancing. I was sitting in an armchair in the corner. Next to me, on the floor, Ashton was drinking in silence. Did he feel ill at ease? When he drank a stillness spread over his features till they became stone-cut. A waxy paleness as the evening advanced.

"Would you care to dance?" Dinos asked.

We moved tentatively on the floor, searching and retreating, not in tune with each other's reactions. I tripped and we both laughed, then moved together as if the tempo gave us some assurance, faster and faster across the floor, the ceiling swaying, their faces approaching and fading, now closer, now far, far away, floating with the curtains past the open windows, outside in a faint-blue light. My body close to his, a scent of wool in my nostrils, his warmth coming through my velvet dress, my hair brushing his face.

Then the music stopped. I went to drink some water. The physical sensation of his arms still in me, of his clothes, of the smoothness of his hands as he held my arm, strongly. I could feel my eyes burning with a heat that made them shiny.

"I shall wait for you here." He sank smiling in a chair near the door.

The kitchen was silent. My head reflected in all the dark windows. From the drawing room the singer's voice came lost in the foggy lights of a night club, floating above their indifferent faces:

I'm a fool to want you
I'm a fool to need you . . .
I know it's wrong . . . it must be wrong . . .

I drank the water and felt dizzy.

When we left we walked through the resonant streets in the moonlight holding hands. A blue night. We ran through the park, and we laughed for no reason. We stopped in the church door to admire the view over the valley, the light fell on the trees distant and mysterious, and when I looked at Dinos, his face had closed in, frozen, absorbed, and his lips came hot and direct on my

THE ISLAND

mouth, releasing all the nerves that had been winding up in me in a knot. At his touch the tension flew into the ground and I rose free, full of a silent fever that burnt off my senses and left me full of space and carelessness.

"My love . . . my love . . ."

I watched him seriously as the words rushed past, trying to absorb his features, the light in his eyes, the shape of his neck, the words that his skin had to tell, the movement of his hand lifting my fingers to his lips.

And we walked down the familiar road unconcerned, touching each other like blind people discovering each other for the first time. I turning round and round in this whirlpool of offering, this richness of offering that burdened me, excited me, made me feel guilty, demanded my attention, this offering that shaped me anew and in which I turned totally without defence.

"Darling . . . darling . . . I love you so much . . ."

I came down the steps unseeing. There was still a light in Aunt Niki's room.

"Is that you, Melina?"

"Yes, Aunt Niki."

I did not want to see anyone. I felt dishevelled and exposed. Everything was probably written on my face. I stayed in the doorway, glad that the bedlamp was dim.

"You are late."

"Mr. Nemours gave a party for us after the performance—I will tell you tomorrow . . ."

My voice sounded extravagant, I tried to bring it to a more normal pitch. I went to have a shower, wash the unfamiliar away, return to normal. But his words

ANTIGONE KEFALA

jumped in the room, in the light, in my ears, stared at me from the mirror, all these coloured lights, all this flow of images that changed me, falsified me into a person I was unable to recognise, to identify with . . .

" . . . you have the most beautiful eyes I have seen . . ."

. . . Like an incantation, I kept repeating the magic words . . .

let me live for you
let me love you forever . . .

Across the dinner table Loula's mother smiled sweetly at me, her raw coffee-bean eyes, honeyed and still as in a painting in which a mellow summer light fluttered. I offered her the bread.

"My treasure," she said turning to Loula.

My treasure, I repeated inwardly, what beautiful expressions Greek had, I was just discovering, like Dinos's words—*my whole being is full of you* . . .

They were noisy around the table, questioning Christos, Loula's brother who had just returned from a holiday in Greece and had brought to dinner a visiting archimandrite. A young, strongly built man, full of a barbarous energy, like Father's, with dark-brown glossy eyes and a good laugh, very quick-witted, raising laughter around the table with his "When the devil has nothing better to do, he annoys the monks." He spoke of the church as "the Bride of Christ," his whole vocabulary full of these sensual images, "adorned like a bride," "modest like a bride" . . . This ideal bride they

THE ISLAND

all seemed to be dreaming about, a static, beautiful, divine, unattained thing that filled the scriptural texts.

I watched them all, strangely disconnected, too preoccupied inwardly. I pretended to be interested in the discussion from time to time, so that they would not notice, but I wanted them all away, an empty space around me in which I could repeat to myself the entire story from the beginning, starting from the dance, stretching the first part so that I could feel again the surprise of the first words. I could not remember them exactly, but repeated them over and over again, in an effort to absorb them, to make them a part of me, to convince myself.

When they all got up to farewell the archimandrite, I drifted out too, pretending that I was going to help with the dishes, but instead walked through the house and into Loula's room, and stretched on the bed.

The whole room was white and empty, only on the dressing table a snapshot of Miki and Loula, somewhere under a palm tree, holding each other and laughing, their faces turned upwards towards the sun that seemed to be raining light on them.

What would Dinos say tomorrow? I tried to imagine. How would we face each other.

I felt so unfamiliar, as if my old, plain self had suddenly been replaced by a very daring, sensual version that excited me with its foreignness. It was as if my image in his eyes came back to possess me, to obsess me, yet at the same time the implications were too frightening in their unknown depths to be analysed. From the dining room the voice of the singer drifted slowly through the house—

48

how much I love you
only I know . . .

—those mirages of love and desire that filled the air. When we left, the dawn was breaking, everything covered in a clean, cold light. We walked down the street towards the beach. The street and the houses still asleep and at the corner a milkman running, the bottles chiming.

The sea was still dark, lead-coloured. Across the stark, open line of the horizon, small black clouds had gathered in rows against the light-blue sky. Then the seagulls stopped flying, and across the waters a deep silence settled as if nothing was alive; the waters did not move, nor the wind, transfixed, as the clouds became slowly orange, darker and darker orange. I had left them to come down to the beach. The rocks were cold, blue-grey, and the waves hardly moved as if the depth was holding its breath, walking on tiptoe.

And then above the line of the clouds an enormous orange disk emerged. It stood there suspended for what seemed to be an interminable time, and then as if turning, light streamed out of it, incandescent light gushed across the waters, flowed like fine strands of hair, brilliant dust exploding on the waves making the entire surface live with spangles. The beach stretched like an arm full of white sand and further in the transparent stream a fisherman was waiting petrified. The rocks had turned into warm browns and the sea came breaking against the rocks, a deep sound as if the earth responded from its

THE ISLAND

very depths, and the white crystal foam leapt higher and higher, dissolved in the light till one could not tell what was light and what was sea.

Everything seemed so untouched, so new, the morning of the world. Oh! I felt like singing, running, embracing all this sparkling immensity. My voice echoed across the waters towards them: "What magnificence!"

I felt that the past had been so small, so narrow, so mean. This morning it seemed to me that the earth contained only riches, riches which were offered so nobly, so naturally, with such ease.

This was what we were trying to reach, in our innermost hearts, this slow burning of all the opaqueness in our bones, till we became transparent like the light. Till we could dissolve in this brilliant mist, walk across the satin, studded waters, a mirror reflecting only light.

The late sun flowed steadily through the lean gothic windows. He was lost somewhere in the depths of the lecture room, his voice came unreal and monotonous through the particles of chalk that moved restlessly in the light.

He was analysing the nineteenth century, his mind full of facts, names, minor happenings, but out of this nothing emerged. His nineteenth century remained as closed to one as before. What an obsolete machine the intellect seemed to be. It moved along the roads of time, cracking, full of chains, puffing at each step, rigid, and in order to change direction it had to stop and readjust itself, limited always by a linear potential. A perpetual anachronism. Our entire lives governed by this obsolete instrument that tried forever to measure and adjust, stubbornly postulating static insights to which we persistently clung with desperation, not to be left in an unmapped country.

I took all the details down, restless with the whole exercise. Ashton was next to me entering everything in his upright writing in his large notebook. I could cut his face out by moving my head lower over the page, so that my hair fell between us and screened me like a curtain. I could never rest in his presence. From time to time he made some incredible gesture that touched you because of its rarity and the effort it must have taken him to do it, as on the afternoon when he bent suddenly to touch my hair in the afternoon sun that was flowing through us. The lightest, most delicate of touches, to tell me how alive my hair was. And then he went on looking at me with his blue-green eyes, as if he had risen above himself and for the moment felt at ease.

We seemed to be spending a lot of afternoons together, travelling from lecture room to lecture room, listening to the new lecturer who spoke on courtly love. He was tall and heavy with a rich voice that rose out of the dark resonances of his stomach, flowering through his throat, a slightly self-obsessed voice, as if unable to free itself from the fascination of sounds. He had just returned from overseas where he had spent eight years studying the subject in the vaults of famous libraries. He

THE ISLAND

spoke with great eloquence, describing the finest refinements of the game, trying to impress on us that the idea of love, like all major and vital ideas in science and art, was not a static one, but had changed throughout the centuries, carrying with it every part of the human body, and changing people's attitudes to it. He would say, for instance, that what would have constituted a lover's delight in one century would have made one from another age totally miserable. And as an example he quoted from a medieval tale in which the heroine's breasts were compared to walnuts.

The whole class laughed uneasily, uproariously at this. I laughed too, but I was preoccupied, restless. I found everything superfluous, all this paper analysis that prepared us for nothing. If I looked around, at all the displayed relationships, on the lawns, in the classrooms, at parties, I could see nothing but physical gestures that engaged no one, a continuous change of partners, as if personalities were immaterial. A physical squandering, repetitive and pointless, as if they were not aware of the potency of their bodies, movements that had no weight. Was I the only one aware of the immutable laws that physical gestures carried their own fate too, imposed on you by a careless abuse, a reality that was not your own and that finally you could not escape. This fatality inherent in our gestures no one took any notice of. Not even Dinos, who since that evening had disappeared.

He was nowhere.

Neither at the coffee shops where I used to meet him by chance so often before, nor at the cable car, where he

ANTIGONE KEFALA

seemed to be arriving just as I came down from a lecture, nor in the cafeteria—to surprise me, as he said. He was nowhere. And I listened, listened continuously, listened all the time to steps, in the corridors, in the streets, at the bus stops, listened listlessly now, walked vacantly and tried to cope with everyday life so that no one would notice.

Yet I was afraid to see him now for he had grown to an amazing size. All the burning energy of my mind had concentrated on him and each day that fell between that evening and now had transformed him into a large lifeless body that filled my mind, growing day by day, pushing everything out. A lifeless doll that performed with a mechanical accuracy the same acts, said the same words. Everything had transformed into a ritual that I repeated over and over again.

The outline was fading already, his face nebulous, and the words which had branded my mind with their sharpness were losing their shape, eaten away by too much handling. I was afraid to see him now, like an addict who waits for a drug that promises a release, but which I knew would create another tension. And the hours dragged on and on, and now I hoped that the day would stretch so that each enlarged second could last longer, give him time to come, and now that the night would come quickly, so that I could sleep and forget.

Yet the nights were full of dark, agitated dreams. The night before I was dreaming that I was at home, I had been walking for days searching for something, and I was tired and thirsty. It was nighttime, in some unknown

THE ISLAND

streets of the old city, I did not remember them, the air was blue, indigo-blue-white, as if the light of the moon passed through a fine purple mesh before reaching the air. I was walking alone in these cobblestoned streets, whitewashed walls and houses stretching endlessly, livid and silent, closed shutters, arrested in the moonlight.

It must have been in the very dead of night. My steps sounded hollow and dry on the pavement. Then they became prolonged, as if another step was added to mine. Someone was following me. The air stirred behind me and the steps could be heard clearly eating the air in large gulps.

I started to walk faster and faster and as I turned a corner, the first corner, an immense black shadow fell over the wall like the wings of a bird spread out, with a small round head towering above, and I started to run, my heart beating faster and faster. The moon ran in the sky before me, gliding behind the clouds blown by an unfelt wind.

And then I saw the church. There it was rising in the distance, if only I could reach it I would be safe. I made gigantic efforts to run but did not seem to move at all, only the moon ran in the sky, and in a last agonising effort I found myself on the cold steps. I lay there, my face hidden in my arms, and slowly the beating of my heart became more quiet. And when I looked up, the houses had receded in the distance and the church stood in the middle of a large square paved with enamelled tiles, brilliant in the moonlight, glistening like frost crystals.

The bell of the church struck in the empty square and I turned and walked inside.

I made the sign of the cross as I entered. I was at home, at St. Constantine. I stood there taking in the lean darkness of the arches and the dome, the round pillar where I used to come with the school during Holy Week. Everything was so peaceful, the familiar scent of hot wax and incense filled the air, and under the icons the oil lamps burnt in their silver chalices. Everything was there, untouched, unchanged, as if I had been away for only a day.

But as I turned from the corner to walk towards the altar, there in the middle of the darkness a coffin rose on a dais, lighted by two white candles burning at each end. I was sure that it had not been there when I had come in, but did not question it, as if its appearance was entirely justifiable.

Around, the pews were full of people watching by the dead, their closed faces masks suspended in the candlelight. I advanced slowly, knowing that they were all watching me, mounted the rug-covered steps of the dais, and bent down to kiss the icon. Dinos was there, stretched in the coffin in his brown tweed suit. I touched his forehead and in that second he opened his eyes and smiled.

Smiled mockingly . . .

He was probably smiling mockingly all these days. He was indifferent. Words had no meaning for him, neither had his gestures. It was probably a sort of refrain he sang to every woman . . .

let me love you for ever . . .

THE ISLAND

He was saying to Alexi one evening that women were very naive.

"They are sending you flowers now," Mina said, laughing, pointing to the flowers on the table. An enormous bunch of blue irises. "Another admirer, do I know him?"

My heart had stopped. They must be from Dinos. There must have been a reason why he had not come. He wanted to surprise me. I was flooded with warmth at the thought.

I watched the small, elegant writing on the blue card. Max Newman! My mind had gone blank. Max Newman—who was he?

"Do you know a Max Newman?" I asked Mina. Then it suddenly came to me, the baby-blue man from the Vegetarian Restaurant.

I stood at the window and watched the night and the tall pines rising from the valley towards the lights and the houses. The warm, intimate houses on the hill, houses that protected people, protected them all, gathered them in the light of the windows.

I was alone as always. Alone in this dark night, in this dark valley. Empty.

I could never find someone to share this loneliness. I knew it tonight with a certainty that cut my body with the sharpness of a knife. This longing that I felt continuously for someone in whose presence I could rest, feel warmth, feel at home, love, be friends with . . . I would always be alone. Lost among strangers, their voices came from the dining room as from a faraway country. They were all busy talking, they laughed and their laughter hurt.

I went out and walked slowly between the trees, my eyes full of tears breaking down my cheeks, warm and salty, and I let them run in a desire to point out to them all, the night and the trees and the sky, how unhappy I was. And the creek flowed, its sharp desolate sound running through the pebbles, and the rundown bridge looked hopelessly fragile.

I crouched against the bridge cold and numb. And I stayed there till I could not feel my body any longer, till between my tears and the flowing creek there was no dividing line, lost in an empty land, walking forever alone with nowhere to rest my head. I had no one. They were all far away, indifferent. I rocked myself as I used to when I was a child, rocked myself to make my mind sleep, not to think any longer.

Saturday night. The most advertised night of the week, the night of adventure, romance, a night out of the ordinary, a night everyone discussed the rest of the week, analysed, a night that songs had been written about.

Through the bus window the streets were dark. Slowly they were gathering in front of picture theatres, at corners, going forward to dances, a brashness about the crowds, noisy, exaggerated. All those couples that

THE ISLAND

one did not notice during the week, the young men much too stiff, like country boys in town for the fair, and the girls much too painted, the bus was full of them, with black-rimmed eyes, blue-white iridescent eyelids, rouged cheeks, crayoned mouths in heavy colours, eyelashes heavy with mascara. Girls my age, hardly out of school, wearing heavy masks that transformed them into Saturday night symbols, as if dividing themselves from their everyday lives with high-heeled shoes, long splits in their dresses, an imagined sensual adventure to which they were aspiring with desperation, but which they still could not sustain.

I looked out of the window feeling very old. As far as I could remember I had never been young, carefree, always weighed down with problems, responsibilities, constantly afraid. The thought of yet another week, another month, at the University seemed unbearable. That closed space bending over tables in the library, the books cold, old and morose, waiting in their prisons, laid next to each other. There was no future anywhere.

"Are you all right?" Aunt Niki kept asking.

"Yes, fine."

You must discipline yourself! I kept saying savagely to myself in the mirror every morning. You will never be able to achieve anything if every small thing unbalances you so quickly! Waiting so many days for Dinos to come, your entire life can go past, and you will still be waiting.

A cold wind was blowing as I came out of the bus. People were rushing, coming out of their cars in great trepidation, buttoning their coats, their eyes and the direction of their senses magnetically drawn towards the club, the building alive with lights and amplification, so that it did not matter from what direction they were coming, the angle was established immediately they hit the cold air. Past the parking lot, men dressed in yellow mackintoshes were making friendly remarks about the weather, the traffic.

The theatre was still empty, with the slightly tattered brown velvet curtain down. The whole place was faded, the paint flecking. But the air warmed up as more people began to enter and, the lights went up. Then the advertisements started. Everything in giant sizes, constantly inflated voices that talked about size as if obsessed by it. And on the screen, a galaxy of ice creams, sausages, frankfurters, and chickens smiled self-assured like over-fed babies floating in strange, powerful lights. Finally the darkness descended on us all, soothing, and we settled into it with a sigh.

The stark images of the film and the resonance of Russian filled the air. The dome of the cathedral appeared and inside through the stained-glass windows, the light came flowing like the tail of a comet, tainted with the brilliant colours of the glass. The place was full of dark, powerful faces, the language rang flamboyant over the steppes covered in snow on which his shadow travelled. And the space echoed the stark lines of his face and his dream that seemed boundless. An intoxication with space and with power. But each image, as it came, was perfectly caught. An artistic sense had burnt away every

THE ISLAND

wastage to leave only this prismatic shape that exploded like a crystal.

I felt so much alive, as if I had woken from a deep sleep. I stretched in the seat to feel my skin. I took a deep breath. Nothing could trap me any longer. The lights had come on, and I was impatient to be away from them all and out into the free air.

"Melina," he said and touched me.

I forced my way through the crowd, trying to escape. But he was following stubbornly and caught my arm as I was coming out into the street.

"Why are you running?"

"I am not."

"Yes you are."

We walked in silence.

"How did you like it?"

"Marvellous," I said in a defiant voice that echoed the hero, echoed the proud lines of his face and his scorn of traitors. "Yes, quite nice."

His voice was normal, the gestures casual. We went towards the bus stop through the park. The fountain was on. The water leapt up in the air, higher and higher, dissolving in phosphorescent colours against the night sky. Through the curtain of images that filled my mind he came as from a faraway country.

"I could not find you anywhere the entire week. Were you at your parents' place?"

He was lying, covered it with a casual, eager air acquired through years of practice. He knew I was angry and went along coaxing me, slowly, putting the right amount of flattery and the right amount of doubt, and here and there a strong note of love, but only for a second, to see what the response would be, and in front of my determined, hostile silence he performed again the entire gamut of his tricks, in a flow of words to confuse and gain time, and then he used his comic repertoire, pretending that he was a man walking on a tightrope, imitating the movements that he knew had made me laugh.

I watched him seriously, trying to resolve the problem, reach a decision, explain to myself his indifference to an entire week of misery. Now I could see that the restlessness had been only in me. This extraordinary reaction to his words, his touch that had thrown everything inside in such a turmoil, did not apply to him somehow.

His reactions came alive only when in contact with me, an excitement that was skin-deep, when the outside impulses ceased there was very little left, at any rate nothing that would disturb his days. He was foreign tonight. I felt no relation to him any longer. All the richness of the previous evening had gone.

But as we sat down at the table in the coffee shop, under the low lights, the touch of his hand had remained the same, everything reduced in the end to this physical level. A sophistry of some kind.

PART III

The proprietor of Vera Cruz was Mexican. A tall, handsome woman, mellow skinned, her head could be seen in the dimness of the restaurant, lost among the smoky lights, like a black shiny jewel, her hair tight in a rich coil, the heavy earrings dangling from her ears, her black eyes lost in the distant country from which her husband was supposed to be coming. Her name was Mrs. Blasco, like Blasco Ibáñez of *The Four Horsemen of the Apocalypse* that Mother had read as a girl and had been very impressed with. The image of her legs, her body, mingled in my mind with those of Alexi, suntanned and sculptured, coming out of the sea at night, shimmering with water in the blue light of the moon. An effect achieved by the glossy, coloured photographs of Mexico that covered the walls of the restaurant.

They were friends, Alexi had told Anna, and went for swims together. She had a house near the sea, an old magnificent house full of carved furniture, all brought out of Mexico, the garden full of exotic shrubs, and a lawn that advanced into the sea. And she gave marvellous parties. Anna was jealous. The Mexican was definitely more experienced than she was, she was telling me, and, being married, had nothing to lose if she lived with him.

In the semidarkness of the place, I watched the slim figure of Anna in her black coat and the long flowing hair moving through the tables towards us, and wondered how could she still love Alexi when she knew all this. How could she continuously absolve him of any responsibility, as if Mrs. Blasco was to blame, as if it were a temporary arrangement before some final, permanent heroic happening that would absolve him.

Relationships, I felt, were absolute things, leaving no room for someone else, possessive things. I could not grasp this practical approach, this settling for less, for a piece, however small, of someone's attachment. Relationships were gifts, either a total gift, or nothing.

Yet here I was, as cowardly as Anna. Why did I keep on seeing Dinos? There was no future in the relationship, I knew it well. I was not moved inwardly by him, flattered but unmoved. Something else was required to stir me, to bind me deeply, to win my loyalties, something which he did not have. And yet his gestures placed me under a constant obligation from which I could not free myself. I seemed to suffer constantly from this guilt, as if any show of warmth, or affection, however superficial, placed me under an obligation to respond. And yet, I could not find an adequate form for the response. I had not yet learnt to accept things as they were but was forever labouring after every gesture, wanting to change it, take it a step further or stop it somewhere else.

This enormous obligation Dinos was placing on me, an obligation that excited me but which at the core had a chilling effect. His face kept coming back at me, bending down to kiss me, the touch of stone on his face, which was no longer his, but some concentration from inside that totally absorbed him, an inward-turning eye that was blind to anything but itself, as if the thing had taken possession of him, sucked him out, so that he, Dinos, the Dinos of everyday, was no longer there, something that emptied him of his personality, reduced him to certain reactions which were repetitive, indifferent. A stranger came out of him, and when the stranger went away there was a moment of awkwardness in the air, which we tried to cover, disconcerted, both trying to find again our usual selves.

But I was forcing myself not to ask too many questions. I went with the tide. A film on Fridays, joining him at Vera Cruz where he had his meals every night, sometimes with Alexi, sometimes with Bebe, the guitarist with the face of a Byzantine icon and the red shirt. His dark eyes melted every time he looked at me.

I watched Dinos eating. He sat down as if doing something important, that one should give due consideration to, yet not exaggerated, just right. One's bread, one's salad, one's fried fish, a straightforward relationship with a simple, clean thing, that was important while he was at it, but cut immediately he finished. He ate with concentration, silently, moving between the dishes, sometimes discussing, but mostly preoccupied with the food. When he finished he rested pleased, looked around, lighted a cigarette. He was free to move to the next thing.

Bebe ate haphazardly, preoccupied, distracted by the latest record of Sotiria Bellou singing rembetika, a marvellous thing he had only just got hold of. That husky, broken voice came back at you with some unimagined, dark quality that moved you beyond words. He kept complaining at the lack of intensity in all of us. "Eating too much," he kept saying, "We are all eating too much" . . . too much beef, too much of everything, our spirit will dry out, enmeshed in this fat, everything too easy, nothing could come out of this, this was not a country for musicians, the only language they spoke here was of beef and cattle, and the price of wool, and how to eradicate rabbits and myxomatosis, no one has yet invented a sound for these things. This was why he could no longer play. What could the guitar do? What language could it speak. All resonance had gone.

He took out the guitar to demonstrate.

"Listen to this sound, see how stubbornly it refuses to say anything?" Dinos laughed.

"Come, come Bebe. What about other sources of inspiration?"

He began to hum softly the popular song:

I tasted you my girl mouthful by mouthful like the wine . . .

Bebe blushed.

"You see," he said to me, "one can't discuss serious things with him." Quite late, when the place was almost empty, with Alexi and Anna there and a few people who had come after the pictures for a coffee, Bebe began to play, and as we all warmed up, we began to sing, the place suddenly full of this sheer resonance that I had almost forgotten, that carried you, responded to you immediately, in an exchange which was so much a part of you and in which you felt at home.

And I was suddenly advancing in this sea of marble dust, up and down the winding streets full of white glistening rocks, with my satchel, harsh passionate voices drifting from the small cafes above the click of the backgammon, black figures waiting in front of the whitewashed walls, the light platinum silver, and from the top, the hills on the other side, floating on a sea of transparent light.

When I reached the Town Hall, Dinos was waiting on the steps looking well in his dark costume and new haircut, which gave his neck a vulnerable look.

I was in high spirits. Professor Stevens had liked the essay, minus A, full of complimentary remarks in the margins. I could see in Dinos's face that I was beautiful tonight. I felt well in Aunt Niki's black velvet coat, an adventurous woman going out for the evening with a man. I moved down the aisle between the seats and laughed. Beautiful and foreign, I could feel it in their eyes. Dinos followed, full of solicitude, as if escorting a celebrity.

THE ISLAND

On the stage, the musicians began to enter one by one, settle down in their places, speak to each other, and tune their instruments, a large family, at ease with one another. The visiting Czech Philharmonic. Their black evening suits, their patent leather shoes, reminded me of European paintings—Degas . . .

The conductor came and the concert started. The musicians preoccupied, waiting for their next entrance, full of tics, stretching their necks, adjusting their violins, their bows, their faces, their eyes full of inner monologues, their past lives, their present worries, the stage full of the atmosphere of their lives. Maybe I imagined it, their backgrounds, which they were continuously confronting, arguing with, in between snippets away from the music, to fall into it again, as in a sea that swept them away, then brought them back to stillness for a few minutes, coming back to the tempo, the cellos looking like golden totem poles bathing in electric suns, the brass at the back, and the bells, exotic primitive silver gods waiting to be touched.

Then I forgot them as the drums struck suddenly under an open sky to announce the beginning of the world. The music came smashing in the blazing whiteness of the lights, lamenting, falling in love with its own image, singing of love, of a past love, of a remembered love, now coming through countless veils of silk. It fell and rose in a frenzy of sound and energy, savage, possessed, recognising nothing but its own power which intensified, consuming itself, sweeping in its movements all the musicians, the instruments, the lights above the podium, rising continuously to explode suddenly in the drums.

The lights were on. We were all up, clapping, smiling at each other. There were shouts from the back, the conductor returned, overwhelmed, bowed again and again, the orchestra rose with him. We drifted slowly out of the hall. Curtains of light hung all around me, through which I advanced, protected from everything.

We had come into the newly opened restaurant to have supper. The crockery was blue white, and in the middle of the table there were two small pearl-pink roses surrounded by delicate ferns. The place was full of couples gazing into each other's eyes, holding hands, drinking expensive wines, at their best, involved in continuous inner discussions with themselves, laughing with an exaggerated edge, too flamboyant for ordinary occasions, forced on them by the adventure, by the unreal situation, by exciting proximities, by fear. A "courting atmosphere," if one were to use an old expression, presided over by two Frenchmen, silent with smiling eyes, changing dishes with easy movements.

While above us the froggy voice of the singer came, hoarse, desperate, lost in a labyrinth of agony . . .

Et pourtant . . . pourtant . . . Je n'aime que toi . . .

I felt uneasy, but Dinos was at home. He looked around full of interest, at the tables, the women, the decor, greedy to catch everything, avid lest something escape him. He engaged in a quiet banter with the Frenchman, his hands touching mine across the table, watching me with dark glossy eyes.

As the evening advanced, he drank a little, became full of stories, all most of them about well-known figures at home, mostly womanisers it seemed, their life's adventure being measured by the number of women they had had. They adored this instinct, wearing it around their necks, pointing at it, all a boys' club, measuring themselves by it. I had never heard him speak like this before, this was a side of him that he had obviously been very careful to screen from me. Yes, he spoke of women as having the best time. When young, playing the game to their advantage, getting married, having children, being supported. When old, being revered and feared as witches. He had moved his chair around so that he could embrace me from time to time, give me a gentle kiss on the hair, then he moved away, uncertain, as if he could not find the right place to settle, whether he would be allowed to settle.

And I listened, laughed from time to time, a laughter which he said provoked him even more. I was slowly dissociating myself from him. I had already become sociable. I had nothing to do with him and with his hunting game. He seemed to imagine me an easy prey, the implications were his, not mine, it was as if I were picking up all these directions from inside him. He thought that a medium performance would do, the best one kept for more important issues.

I was tired. I wanted to go home. The place was suffocating with an implied menace. I watched him drink

ANTIGONE KEFALA

another glass, till his gestures became more and more extravagant, his entire vocabulary against me, women, as a game that had to be won, to be discarded, to be enjoyed, to be discussed. He kept telling me that all men were children looking for a mother. Then he quoted the French saying, "A woman must be a cook in the kitchen, a lady in the drawing room, and a prostitute in bed." I watched him with steely eyes.

"I must go home, Dinos," I said, "I am very tired," my voice savage with anger.

He looked at me with vague eyes, taken aback, hurt. He gathered himself together, shrank slightly, put on a sociable face, called the waiter, ordered a taxi.

Before falling asleep, I watched for a long time the water in the glass on my bedside table—its absolute rightness, its absolute balance, its vulnerability; the light caressing the water with the hands of a lover, the transparent shades that stirred in it, as if trembling lines. The whole thing moved me. I was afraid for it, a fragile, marvellously balanced, beautiful thing that could not possibly last.

Lives spent in libraries, all of us bent over the same tables, absorbed, as if for the last few months we had not moved from here. I was trying to cheer myself by looking at a book of photographs of Greece that Kate had discovered. There it was, page after page, arrested forever, the delicate transparent feeling of the landscape,

THE ISLAND

the sun pouring white over the crumbling architecture of the buildings and the streets, the dark weight of the people, women statically bent over the fields.

Grandmother Sofia was there too, eternally waiting on a bench in the Zappeion. The same fine-boned face under the small hat, her eyes, and that brittle feeling, as if a leaf that had been pressed for many years between the yellowed pages of books. I remembered her only in summer. I would watch her from the gate turning the corner, a small, thin, black-clad figure moving swiftly, the pleats at the bottom of her skirt agitating along the white walls, coming through the haziness of heat. I would run to tell mother. She would settle in a chair against the drawn curtains, in the coolness of the rooms, take out of her bag a sparkling-white lace-trimmed handkerchief to dust her face.

Outside, the heat of summer would break against the walls, buzz in the windows, hiss in the air, but inside, Grandmother Sofia went on unhurriedly unfolding the silk thread of her peace, cool as the water brought in with the sweets, spinning it around . . .

"Most lives are anachronistic," Aunt Niki was saying the night before. "We all live in accordance with attitudes, concepts, that are five, ten, twenty years old. The present takes time to make an impact. And when it does, how many people are putting any effort into updating their truths . . ."

She was in a great mood. A Mr. Svoronos had arrived for dinner, a friend from the old days. Loula was there too, looking better. But the star of the evening was Aunt

Niki. She looked refined, with that handsome head and Grandmother Sofia's marvellous earrings, gold filigree, sitting on her ears as if elaborate feathers.

She traced slowly her inner argument, speaking seriously, as I had not heard her before, of very intimate issues, as if the company was worth it, as if all of us around the table had released this feeling of companionship in which she could speak freely.

". . . Look at me wearing my berets, when no one here wears berets, having coffee in the friendliest coffee shops I can find, trying to buy good bread, reading my European authors. I feel that I am carrying Europe in me, moving in its rhythm, following my mother's and my father's path, a Europe that is probably no longer, as if I am still propelled by a tempo that has been set on its course ten, twenty years ago, to which, from time to time, I have made minor adjustments in response to the new environment, trying to fit them into the pattern as intelligently as possible, so as not to destroy the living body of my life, not to estrange myself from it . . ."

Crossing the street from the University, I felt very cold and put up the collar of my coat. From the other side of the street Mrs. Blasco was coming, her deep-red coat matching the colour of her lipstick. She stopped to chat, very sociable, suddenly full of friendliness and an ill-disguised curiosity. She had not seen me at the shop for some time and wondered how I was. Was everything all right? I must come with her and see her house, have a cup of coffee. One of Dinos's friends had just arrived and was staying with her, it would be nice if we could meet. By the time I could think of an excuse we were already in her car and travelling. The traffic heavy, school children noisy, listless, and bored waiting everywhere at bus stops, while the afternoon was falling over the rough lawns, humid and cold.

We went down rock-carved steps through the garden and passed a tall, rather shaky man working among the shrubs. The house was brown brick, humid inside and very dark, one of those houses built in the thirties, the forties, graceless and square, with a feeling of heaviness everywhere. It was difficult to believe that Mrs. Blasco would have chosen such a house to live in. Her presence had made no impact.

Dinos's friend was there, in dark-blue corduroy trousers and a short sports jacket, white hair and heavy sensual lips. I was in a dreadful mood, angry that I had been forced to come, not feeling well, coming out of myself with difficulty. I did not want to see either of them, or speak to them. I was annoyed that they were forcing me to respond. Something made me uneasy, but I could not decide what it was. Dinos's friend spoke constantly of himself, his wife, his children, his grown-up children, of his years in Mexico (he was an archaeologist), of his writings, his discoveries, a satirical, sometimes cruel angle to all his opinions. I would not have liked to have him as a friend.

He spoke of Dinos, his second cousin, how Dinos had spoken of me. He kept on having to go to talk on the telephone, to friends, he said, acquaintances, while I waited among the large bronze vases full of aspidistras (if they were not aspidistras, they became like them in that atmosphere). Mrs. Blasco was preparing coffee. Through the large windows I could see the valley full of red tiled roofs, and further the hills with a heavy, crematorium-like chimney. A depressing sight, the evening sun falling humid and brick red on everything. I assumed that the sea must have been on the other side.

We finally all sat down to drink coffee, while he bent conspiratorially to tell me, "Dinos likes you very much," the tone unreal. What message was he giving me that I was unwilling to receive. The message sounded fake on his lips and I rejected it. I responded in the same unreal tones, "And I like him too," as if the matter was very light, and had no need to be discussed. He came back to the message again, with some insistence.

"Dinos has wanted us to meet."

What message was he waiting for, what did he want to take back? I was indifferent. Whatever there was to tell, Dinos and I should be able to say it to each other directly. I was annoyed at his intrusion, at her intrusion.

Finally, I got up to go. They both came through the dark house full of brown furniture and wetness and saw me to the door. I went up into the empty street full of trimmed lawns. On the opposite side a girl was walking bored in a garden, the dusk falling on the wintry shrubs, the houses waiting uninterested, and the trees, their arms cut off, shivering in the wetness.

I stayed there leaning on the brick wall till the bus came, then got in quickly, low-spirited and tired. My soul was made of humid lead and it refused to move, and

THE ISLAND

I sank with it, lower and lower, uninterested. I was cold, a snow-like chill at the very depth of my bones, as if a cold line had been traced in my innermost being, and my throat was burning.

As if rising from a long illness, still without a feeling of good health. Very tired of people and of life. Reading my last essay, as if written by someone else, a long time ago, someone with more enthusiasm, more energy.

I went to the University today, everyone looked solid. I stayed in the tutorial and felt as if I were made of glass, every word seemed to shatter me, and I had to put myself together again, the effort unbearable. When I came down through town, the moon was in the dark sky, mysterious.

The trees in the park were breathing in the night. I felt suddenly that I had not been out for a long time. The whole city looked unknown, the Friday streets full of shadows, people full of hidden secrets, rich voices, fantastic lives, laughing together, going towards exotic destinations . . . while I was alone . . .

Kate in the tutorial—was I coming to the Festival at the Cape? "Come, come," she kept urging, "shall I buy you a ticket? Ashton is coming, and so is Michael, and lots of others. It will be fun, just like last year . . ."

No, I was not feeling strong enough to face all that. And thinking of last year . . .

. . . I had reached the ship early. The decks were

ablaze with lights and people. Voices that tried to rise from the dock above the noise and be understood, endearments trying to stretch over the gap that was already forming.

It was not dark yet. A transparent, rich indigo blue enveloped everything. The lights crystal cut, and people advanced in and out of this blueness like shadows. I felt lost among all that exaggerated joy around me. Then they all came on deck, full of noise, their long woollen scarves bearing our colours thrown in the air. They all talked excitedly, as if the night and the journey held unexpected, marvellous promises. I laughed too. My voice laughed but inwardly I was cold. I did not feel at home with them. Outside the familiar university walls they were all unknowns . . .

After dinner we drifted out. There were people everywhere, dancing and singing. We went up, further and further up to watch the sea. The loudspeakers murmuring some indistinguishable song. The bow rose high above the blackness of the waters cutting through the white phosphorescent foam. It seemed as if we were disconnected from the rest of the world, suspended below the dark arch of the sky, on this giant beast that roared from its unimagined depths, bearing us unwillingly on its scaled back, so that in our ignorance we felt safe, deceptively protected, exhilarated by the unleashed force on which we rode.

I was thinking of home, of the first time I had seen the sea, of the silence of the waters then, the silver trail of the moon, shimmering over the expanse. And when

THE ISLAND

we approached the harbour in the early morning, of the walls of mist that surrounded us. Heavy walls of mist that rose on all sides, and we advancing slowly, all of us up on the bridge for the first glimpse of the land. Then suddenly as if a thunder had struck, they began to crumble silently, like enormous walls of granite in a silent movie, and through the cracks, the slightly steamy surface of the sea appeared full of fishermen's boats rocking their lights gently, and in the silence a voice reached across the waters—

Welcome . . . Welcome . . .

like the words of the song . . . . Welcome peace . . .

Then Michael called out that I should sing something. Sing, sing, they all cried, one of those foreign songs. So I sing the old ballad that I had heard on that boat for the first time, sung by those strong-faced men, burnt by the sun and marked by the salty air, their eyes washed out clean. The ballad about the sea and the black-clad mothers. Of sons and lovers lured away by the black beauty covered in white lace, the sorceress with the bewitching heart. Of the roads of forgetfulness that went deeper and deeper, taking away the mind's landscape, and the signs, and the return journey an unmapped dream.

As I turned, above from the mast, the powerful lights exploded in the night and fell on them in bluish arrows. They were grouped around it, still as in a painting, Philip and Jill, Kate and Michael, and Ashton on the other side. And I felt in their eyes an immense pity, a pity for myself, as if there on top of the waves I was burning out in a last effervescence of sound, burnt by a gift that I possessed that could not save me now, a gift that was my doom, that divided me from them, but which was useless.

Then Jill said, "You are such a happy person, Melina," in the same voice that she was to use later in the play. A shrill, metallic voice coming out of the rubbish bin in which she was buried, to beg for a biscuit . . . a biscuit . . .

Ashton was in the play too, a raw, undecided Ashton, his stiff arms and legs interfering with the space, his skin tense. They all ran against this disintegrating background, the light ashen, held together by fear. People who had lost their dignity, their warmth, who did not struggle against fate as the ancients had done, facing it directly.

What plays, my God! What plays! Everyone had forgotten the powerful, intimate connection between art and life, between reality and art, and kept on producing second-rate heroes, that bred around them second-rate people, mean, stubborn, rooted to their rubbish bins, demanding a little charity, however small, however dirty, demanding it stubbornly, for they must have it to chew at on rainy afternoons . . . everything reduced in the end to this small measure . . .

Against the black of his suit Dinos's face looked matte and rested. I liked him tonight. Liked him as a man you watch in the bus or in the street, unknown, pleased with his eyes or his skin. He had gone to buy cigarettes and I watched him crossing the floor, the eyes of girls following him. Alexi was there, talking to Mrs. Kousis, the Modigliani lines of his face accentuated by the white shirt, his long nervous fingers playing with his glass. I wanted him to fall in love with me. Just for one moment.

He got up and asked me to dance. We were both silent. Holding our bodies close, so that my nose reached his shoulder, breathing a faint smell of cigarette and wool. Tighter and tighter the embrace, faster and faster the dance, the floor gliding till our bodies were one, flowing below the chandeliers that moved their prismatic, grape-like bodies, breaking in sparkling lines, then into nebulous suns that turned around and around blinding the featureless faces of the people.

Then the music stopped.

We both moved away and laughed, excited, and as Alexi bent down to protect me from another dancer, I was sure that his lips had brushed against my cheek.

Dinos had returned and was discussing some very serious problem with Anna and, looking at her face, I felt guilty and promised myself not to dance with Alexi any longer.

But the night was mine. Tonight I did not love anyone and yet I loved them all. I smiled in the lights knowing that they liked me. I belonged to no one. I moved my hips, pretending to be a Spanish dancer, just to amuse Dinos, caressed his neck in the dance, smiled secretly at him, at them all, at the world, at my own image that travelled reflected in the mirrors, in their eyes. Tonight

I saw past him, detached. I was there and yet I wasn't. I touched his neck as if I knew the beginning of the sensation and its end and neither made an impression. I looked at him with a detachment that was frightening, as if after so many months nothing had been established between us, as if his eyes, his skin, his movements were all foreign. I felt no attachment to him. I was suddenly alone in the middle of this noise and laughter and I watched their faces, the ballroom, and the tables as if I were an observer.

Around two we left, came out in the street and stopped to discuss, make arrangements for next week, next month. And I waited as if separated from them by years of distance, waited in Aunt Niki's black velvet coat, my dark stockings, my high-heeled shoes, feeling like a wild horse, ready to break out into a gallop. What was I doing there? I made polite conversation with these unknown people, beating my hooves on the dark asphalt, under the electric lights that sparkled between the branches of the trees. Misty. A humid mist was rising.

"Will you be all right?" Mrs. Kousis asked.

"I will take Melina home," Dinos offered.

I wanted so much to go home alone. I felt tired and empty. I did not want to make conversation. I came quickly out of the taxi, hoping that he would stay inside. No, he had already dismissed it. As I turned to go down the steps, he held me close to him, his body stiff, as if made of steel, tense. And as I stepped back to kiss him lightly, the tension broke in a frenzy of trembling that shook his entire body. He groped for my breasts and his

THE ISLAND

hands held my body in a tight, powerful movement, lost in a madness of convulsion. And I was totally lost, did not know what to do, felt only an enormous tenderness towards him, a compassion because I could not respond. I embraced his head and kissed him, the dear boy. It was my fault, all my fault, I tried to give him all the support I could . . .

"Come with me . . . once . . . only once . . ."

"Please Dinos . . . go . . . please go . . ."

The house was asleep. I made some coffee. I felt cold and dirty, my face drawn, and my dress smelt of cigarettes and wine. I felt tired and guilty. Guilty that I had refused him. Ashamed that I played these games and yet refused to accept their full implications. I was false and empty and lacking in courage. For, as he guarded his affections and allowed himself only a surface involvement. I guarded my body and played with it but only up to a point.

I was frozen. I must sleep. Sleep. I forced myself to go that far, touching almost the edge of the empty dark hollowness, but another thought came and I was fully awake and back again with a thief-like movement, but the eye inside was wide awake and refused to sleep.

Then I woke up with a start. The room was silent, I fell slowly back, further and further down, lowered into the air-made mattress, layers of it softly . . .

. . . We were sitting near a bus stop, Dinos and I, late afternoon it must have been, after lectures. A ghost-like tram passed by, full of silent people, in a stillness, as if everything was painted. The houses behind us had a frontage only and between the walls an empty space as in the theatre.

Mrs. Blasco came along wearing a black, camel-hair sweater, the bright earrings dangling from her ears, her lipstick dark red. She insisted that we should go home with her and have a cup of coffee. I remembered that she had asked us before and we had declined, but today we could not think of an excuse somehow, and so we went.

We entered a very old stone house full of vaulted ceilings that underlined the vaulted doors and corridors, and settled in a monastery type of courtyard with fluted pillars. Many people came, all unknown to me. We drank coffee, dark, black coffee, a velvet liquid that had no transparence. I was bored. I took out an embroidery and began to embroider. I imagined that I was in keeping with the closed, sheltered courtyard and the pillars, and the domestic light that filled the place.

Then a man got up and said to an elderly woman, "I will show you the sea."

Now, I was positive that the woman was afraid of the sea. I got up and started to run after them. They had already left the house and were advancing towards the sea, the man behind. I shouted across, "Don't be afraid, the waters are very shallow."

At the same moment the woman stumbled and fell over a rock. There, I said to myself, I should not have said anything, I made her conscious of it. The man had bent down to help her, but as he lifted his arms, he had no arms any longer but wings, colossal wings whose arches spanned from his legs, stretching wide, full of

THE ISLAND

white luminous feathers, transparent, diffused in the last rays of the sun that touched the surface of the sea and broke through them making them disappear in a misty, sparkling, brilliant haze.

I turned towards the house and went in. As I sat down to embroider I realised that the entire house was empty. Empty and silent. Night had come. They must have all gone to the sea. Then someone walked into the house, the steps came from the main entrance towards the hall. It must be her, I thought. But no one came in. Then I heard steps above my head. They stopped. I came out in the corridor and cried, "Is it you, Mrs. Blasco?"

There was no answer. The corridors were dark and somehow all the furniture had disappeared. I ran out, past the vaulted entrance. The sea had gone and instead there was a steep hill covered with gorse. I went painfully up, and as I reached the top, I recognised our street with the houses scattered on the hill.

Three women were waiting at the bus stop. It was so dark at first that I could hardly see their faces. But as I got used to the ink blueness that covered everything, I saw that one of the women was sitting on the bench on which I usually waited for the bus. Her eyes were closed and her face as if petrified. The second woman was listening, frightened, to a girl all dressed in black who was telling her, "Your house will be full of bats that will suck the eyes of your children one by one . . ."

I grabbed the girl's arm and shouted in anger—stop telling her such nonsense, can't you see how frightened she is.

As she pulled away she scratched me with her long, claw-like nails. I pulled her in the middle of the road still holding her arm, while she tried to break free. Her body was covered in a fur-like material, black, deep-night black, sea waters at night, a blackness that emanated magnetic waves. She had a small, dark, yellow face.

She stopped struggling and fixed me with eyes that came out of their sockets, enlarged, burning. Burning with a desire to destroy. My grip got tighter and tighter in my anger, and I fought her with a power that came out of every pore of my body, for in the end there was nothing left but the vision of these two large stones that burnt in the night, bigger and bigger, growing on the darkness, eating away the hills, and the grass and the houses, and that had transformed into fire, a fire that burnt the air hotter and hotter, silently, rising out of the surface of my skin. And then her arm disappeared from my grip, her body was air and the eyes went circling in the current of darkness, a whirlpool of darkness drunk by the top of the hill . . .

The room was silent. The clock ticked and my heart beat madly, faster and faster, still fighting. I got up and looked at the room. Everything was there, the books, the table, my frock on the chair. It was already light. I lay in silence under the bedclothes and tried to warm myself, afraid to close my eyes. I lay there for a long time, breathing deeply.

Then I got up, went to make a coffee, tried to put the image out of my eyes. The kitchen waited clean and arranged as Aunt Niki had left it the night before. Cat heard me and came to the back door. Friendly, watching me silently from the bottom of her eyes, like fluid green marble.

Outside the air was fresh and sharp. The ground covered in hoarfrost. The sun was rising, half caught between houses, the spray of light diffuse. But as I moved down the path it escaped, burst in a shaft that flooded the garden. And near the creek, petrified in the morning silence, the tree spread its branches, dry and cracked like frozen fingers. There it stood, vulnerable and young, glass tears hanging from its arms, each breaking in the light as if a crystal, filling the air with a white resonance.

ANTIGONE KEFALA (1931–2022) was born into a family of musicians in Brăila, Romania, and aspired to be an actor. Following the occupation by the Soviet Union, her family fled Romania, first escaping to Greece and living in refugee camps there. She spoke Romanian, French, Greek, and English, and completed an MA in French in New Zealand after arriving there as an adolescent. Kefala settled in Australia in 1959 and lived in Sydney until her death. She was the author of numerous works of fiction, including *The First Journey*, *The Island*, and *Alexia*, and five poetry collections, *The Alien*, *Thirsty Weather*, *European Notebook*, *Absence: New and Selected Poems*, and *Fragments*, which won the 2017 Judith Wright Calanthe Award and was shortlisted for the Prime Minister's Literary Award for Poetry. Her collections of journals—for which she received critical acclaim—include *Sydney Journals* and *Late Journals*, her final work. She was the recipient of the 2022 Patrick White Literary Award.

MADELEINE WATTS is the author of the novels *Elegy, Southwest* (2025), and *The Inland Sea* (2021), which was shortlisted for the Miles Franklin Literary Award and the Glenda Adams Award for New Writing. She was born and raised in Sydney, Australia. After over a decade in New York, she currently lives in Berlin.

Transit Books is a nonprofit publisher of international and American literature, based in the San Francisco Bay Area. Founded in 2015, Transit Books is committed to the discovery and promotion of enduring works that carry readers across borders and communities. Visit us online to learn more about our forthcoming titles, events, and opportunities to support our mission.

TRANSITBOOKS.ORG